The Revenge of the
Incredible Dr. Rancid and His
Youthful Assistant, Jeffrey

**Other APPLE® PAPERBACKS
You Will Want to Read:**

The Revenge of the Incredible Dr. Rancid and His Youthful Assistant, Jeffrey

by Ellen Conford

AN **APPLE**®
PAPERBACK

SCHOLASTIC INC.
New York Toronto London Auckland Sydney

ISBN 0-590-33746-7

12 11 10 9 8 7 6 5 4 3 2   5 6 7 8 9/8 0/9

Printed in the U.S.A.   11

To David—ideal combination of cheerleader and Simon Legree

The Revenge of the
Incredible Dr. Rancid and His
Youthful Assistant, Jeffrey

One

"Hey, Childish!"

"Ignore him," I told Bix. "He'll stop if you just ignore him."

"But, Jeff, you've been ignoring him, and he isn't stopping."

"Hey, Childish, wait up! What's your hurry? Have to get home to Mommy?"

Bix was right. He's only eight, but he's right a lot of the time. Dewey Belasco wasn't going to stop hassling me just because I ignored him. Dewey Belasco was never going to stop hassling me. I should have been used to it by now. But I wasn't.

My stomach tightened into the usual knot.

"Come on," I muttered to Bix, and walked faster.

Why did my name have to be "Childs"? Why couldn't it have been "Smith" or something? At

3

least then he wouldn't be able to call me "Childish."

But he'd find something else to call me. No matter what my name was. The Dewey Belascos of the world always find a way to get to you.

I shifted into jog. Bix trotted along beside me.

"Aah, go on home, Childish. Everybody knows what a big chicken you are already. You don't have to stick around and prove it."

I passed Lana McCabe and two of her friends. "See you tomorrow, Childish," she said in a singsong voice. One of her friends giggled.

My stomach felt like a clenched fist. It was bad enough that Dewey spent half his waking life bullying me; I could have put up with that if he did it when no one else was around. What did I care what names he called me if no one heard him? But there's no fun in picking on someone unless the whole school hears you do it.

"Why don't you stand up to him, Jeffie?" asked Bix. "He'd stop if you stood up to him."

"If I stood up to him," I said, "I'd reach his chest. And don't call me Jeffie."

I slowed down to a walk again. We were past the crossing guard and I couldn't hear Dewey's voice anymore. My stomach began slowly to unclench.

"You could learn karate," said Bix. "With karate it doesn't matter how big your enemy is."

"What if Dewey knows karate too?"

Bix thought about that for a moment. "He probably doesn't. Big guys never do. They don't think they have to because they're big."

4

"It's only in movies," I said, "that the little guy can beat up the big guy. Believe me, Bix, in real life the little guy always gets mashed to a pulp."

I glanced sideways at Bix. I didn't want to terrify him or anything — I mean, he's only a kid. But on the other hand, it's never too early to learn about the harsh realities of life. I wouldn't be doing Bix any favor if I let him believe that life turns out the way a movie does.

Bix was walking along jerkily, trying to stamp on the loose shoelace of his right sneaker with his left foot as he took each step. He didn't seem especially terrified.

"What about building up your muscles?" asked Bix. He didn't look up from his sneakers. "You could lift weights, and then when you got really strong and muscley —"

"I'd still be a foot shorter than Dewey. And about thirty pounds lighter." I didn't believe any of that body-building stuff would work on me. To begin with, I don't have any muscles at all, so there's nothing to build up. I'm so skinny that — I hate to admit it — I look like I'd crack if somebody sneezed on me. One of those harsh realities of life you have to face is when you're built like me, you're going to spend most of your free time wishing you were built like Clint Eastwood, and the rest of your free time being scared of guys who *are*.

"You want to come home and look at my new cards?" asked Bix. Bix is a very big card collector. Not baseball cards; Bix collects those plastic cards

5

you see advertised on TV. They come with a colored plastic index case, and Bix has cards for just about everything: World War II, Animals of the World, Arts and Crafts — all kinds of stuff.

"What kind of cards?"

"Houseplants. They come in a little greenhouse and everything."

"What do you want houseplant cards for?" I asked. "You don't like plants."

"No. But I like cards."

"Well, thanks anyway, but I don't think so. I've got some stuff I have to do."

"What?" asked Bix.

"Just some stuff." We stopped in front of my house. Bix lives five houses down the block. "I'll see you."

"You coming out later? You want to shoot some baskets or something?" Bix looked hopeful.

Suddenly I got this really sick feeling in my stomach. Here was this little kid, almost three years younger than me, and he was about the only person in the whole world I could really call a friend.

Of course, I didn't ever call him a friend to anybody. He was always just "this kid I know." But the truth was, he was the only friend I had.

There's something wrong with me, I thought. There's really something wrong with me. And it can't just be that I'm afraid of Dewey, because everybody's afraid of Dewey, and he doesn't pick on everybody.

Why me? Why only me? Why *always* me? And why is it that an eight-year-old kid who collects

6

houseplant cards is the only person in the whole world who thinks I'm great?

I sighed deeply. "No. No, I can't come out. I got this stuff to do."

I went into the house, leaving Bix standing on the sidewalk alone.

No one was home yet. My mother is the sports editor of the local paper and usually gets in around four-thirty unless there's a game she has to cover. My father works in the city and doesn't get home till around six-thirty.

I was glad no one was there. If my mother asked me if anything was wrong, I might do something stupid like bust into tears and tell her. And it was bad enough being a skinny coward without being a skinny, *crybaby* coward.

I took some Hawaiian Punch from the refrigerator and poked through the bread drawer till I found a stale Hostess Twinkie. My mother never minds if I eat stuff like Hawaiian Punch and Twinkies because she thinks they'll help me gain weight. But I've been eating Twinkies for nine of my eleven years and they haven't worked yet.

The juice jiggled around in my stomach like cold pebbles. I had this feeling that anything I ate now was going to turn to stone inside me and just lay there, not making me any stronger, just weighing me down. I took a bite of the Twinkie and chewed slowly.

I pictured the crumbs hitting my stomach and beginning to shape back into a solid mass. Now the cream filling — there it went, cementing all the crumbs together, till they re-formed into a Twinkie again — this time, rock hard. Now all the food I ate after this would collect around the Twinkie, making it bigger and bigger until there was a boulder in my stomach.

Then I realized that a boulder in my stomach would certainly make me stick out in front, which was all I needed. ("Hey, Childish, you pregnant or something?") I tossed the rest of the Twinkie into the garbage and went to my room.

I dropped my books on my desk and opened the third drawer from the bottom. I pulled out a notebook from underneath a mess of baseball cards.

I opened the notebook to the first page and looked at the title:

THE REVENGE OF THE INCREDIBLE DR. RANCID AND HIS YOUTHFUL ASSISTANT, JEFFREY

I turned until I came to the first empty page. There was a lot of writing in the book already. I had been working on it for almost a year now. Ever since, in fact, Dewey Belasco had come into my life.

I pulled my pen out of my shirt pocket and chewed on the end of it for a while. Then I began to write.

I could almost feel the rock in my insides dissolving as I wrote. It got smaller and smaller until I finally forgot all about it.

"Jeffie! Jeffie, you home?"
My mother burst into my room without knocking.

8

The door was open, but I don't think that's any reason to invade a person's privacy.

I slammed the notebook shut and stuck it under my math book. Subtle, Jeff, I told myself. She'll never notice that move.

"What's the emergency?" I asked. "And don't call me Jeffie."

"What are you writing?" she asked curiously.

"A composition for English," I lied. "And I asked you first. Why were you so hysterical when you charged in here?"

"I wasn't hysterical, I was just worried. Bertram and the Winchell boys said you were inside and I called and called and you didn't answer. That's all. I was worried that something had happened."

Bertram is Bix. Bertram Bixby is his name, but only my mother and Mrs. Bixby call him Bertram.

"I guess I was concentrating on my composition."

"Didn't you see my note?"

"What note?"

"Ohhh, Jeff. No wonder I didn't smell anything baking."

She stalked out of the room and into the kitchen. I followed behind her. "What note? You didn't leave a note."

"Right here on the kitchen table." She picked it up and tossed it at me. It fluttered to the ground. "Don't you even know what time it is?"

I looked at the kitchen clock. "It's six o'clock. Holy cow, how come you're so late?"

"Read the note," she said icily.

Dear Jeffie: Please start baking potatoes and put

9

*in roast at 425° at 5 PM if I'm not home by then. I
may be late because of away game at Linwood HS.
Turn oven down to 325° at 5:30. Love, Mom.*

She grabbed a bag of frozen french fries from the
freezer and turned on the oven. She reached deep
into the freezer and pulled out a box of frozen
hamburger patties.

"Well, how was I supposed to know you left a
note for me?"

"All you had to do was walk in here. You couldn't
miss it. And there's your dirty glass in the sink, and
your Twinkie crumbs on the table — you *were* in
here — you stood right over the table. You were on
top of that note."

"Brilliant deduction, Holmes. You know all that
from some Twinkie crumbs?"

"Don't be smart with me, Jeffrey. I'm really
annoyed. I work hard all day and I ask you to do a
simple thing like turn on an oven, for heaven's
sakes."

Without thinking — because if I had stopped to
think, I would have cut out my tongue before saying
it — I blurted out, "It's not my job to cook dinner,
it's *your* job!"

She whirled on me, her eyes blazing. I thought
she was going to hit me with a frozen hamburger.
She raised her arm — maybe she was going to hurl
one at me, like a discus thrower. She could have
done it, too — and got me right between the eyes.

"What do you mean, it's not *your* job to cook
dinner? What do you mean, it's *my* job to cook

dinner? I've got a job; your father has a job — and *your* job is whatever we tell you it is. And nobody asked you to cook dinner. I just asked you to turn on the lousy oven, for crying out loud!"

She didn't stop there. She went on screaming for a while. Instead of conking me with the frozen hamburger, she conked me with words.

On the whole, I would have preferred the hamburger.

Maybe if my mother knew about my troubles she would have been more understanding. But since I didn't tell her, since she had never heard the name Dewey Belasco pass my lips, and, since most of the time she treated me like she thought I was a pretty nice kid, she really had no idea that I found her hard to live with.

I didn't mind her working. I thought that was perfectly fine. I didn't need her home at three o'clock to ply me with milk and cookies and questions. In fact, I was just as glad that she wasn't around to see the mood I came home in nearly every day.

But why, of all things, did she have to be a sports writer? And the first woman sports editor in the county? While I, her only son, her sometime — though not this minute — pride and joy, could not even hit a punchball out of the infield. Let alone a softball.

It was ridiculous. She wanted me in the kitchen with an apron, while she ran all over the county covering wrestling matches and hockey games. And what really upset me, what really made my insides churn, was knowing that I *belonged* in the kitchen with the apron, while *she* belonged out there in the front row of the Coliseum, getting splatted with the sweat of grunting wrestlers.

Dewey could have a lot of fun with this little tidbit of information about my mother, if he ever found out about it. So far he hadn't mentioned it, and the only reason I could figure was that Dewey is not one of your heavy readers. But there were other kids who knew, and I was sure it was only a matter of time before Dewey found out. I didn't even want to imagine what Dewey would dream up to hit me with. There are some things man was not meant to know.

"Set the table please, Jeffrey," my mother said coldly. "I believe that *is* one of your jobs."

"Ahh, come on, Mom. I said I'm sorry. Don't keep talking that way." I hate that icicle voice; it's like she puts up this wall between herself and me, and I have to figure out how to knock it down before I can get her on the same side with me again.

She turned to face me. "As a matter of fact, you didn't," she said, her voice softer. "You didn't say you were sorry."

"Well, all right, I am," I mumbled. I had to get past her to get the silverware. She grabbed for me and rumpled my hair and kissed me.

"I'm sorry too, Jeffie. I was tired. I got a little carried away."

I yanked myself free and started grabbing forks

out of the drawer. I don't exactly hate it when she kisses me — but I don't think I want her to know how much I don't hate it.

"And don't call me Jeffie!" I growled.

Two

ey, Jeff, want to shoot some baskets?"
My father half-crouched in the doorway of
my room and dribbled the basketball invitingly.

"Jeffrey, don't bounce that in the house!" my
mother called from down the hall.

"It's not Jeff, it's me," my father called back.

"Spencer, please don't bounce that in the house!"
she yelled.

My father grinned. "She's fair, anyway."

"Oh, yeah? To you she says *please*."

Living with my father is no easy job either. For
one thing, he's not afraid of anything.

I never realized that I was a coward until Dewey
Belasco started after me, and it was then that I
began to notice that my father never seemed to
have the smallest fear about anything.

It's not that he's big and tough and bulls his way

through any situation. He's not particularly big and he doesn't come on like a hit man. It's just this attitude he has, of real self-confidence, like he can take anything that's dished out, handle any trouble that comes along, and never get rattled.

On top of that, he thinks I'm an okay son. I mean, more than okay. He really likes me — not just loves me, but *likes* me. He has no idea that I spend half my life running away from Dewey Belasco. If he did, if he knew what a coward I was, if he knew what I was really like, it would make him sick.

"So? How about it?" My father tossed the ball to me. I caught it just before it hit the wall.

"Sure."

Shooting baskets is one thing I can do. At least, I can do it at home, where the basket is nailed up over our garage. In the gym at school, the baskets are about two feet higher so I'm not nearly as good there as I am in our driveway.

We had a foul-shooting contest, which I won by one basket, and we were just starting a one-on-one when my mother came out of the house carrying her notebook.

"I'm off to the track meet," she announced. "Anyone want to come along?"

"Hey, how about it, Jeff?" asked my father. "You want to go?"

"Nah. I'm not too big on track and field." All those guys running around in their underwear . . .

My father looked disappointed. He dribbled the basketball a few times trying not to show me that he was torn between wanting to go with my mother to the meet and feeling he ought to stay home and spend his Saturday with me, doing good father-and-son stuff.

"Why don't you go, Dad? I have a lot of homework to do anyway." I didn't, but I didn't want him to feel he had to keep me company. "Besides," I added, "Bix said he might want to go to the movies."

"You sure?" he asked doubtfully.

"Sure."

"Well, okay." He perked up right away. "I'll just get my jacket. Catch, Liz!" He tossed the basketball to my mother. She caught it, tucked it under her arm, and walked over to me as my father hurried into the house.

"You'll be okay, Jeff? You don't mind staying alone?"

"I'm alone every afternoon, Ma," I reminded her. "I think I can handle it."

She gave me a little squeeze around the shoulders. "Okay, hon. There's cold cuts in the refrigerator for lunch and some potato salad . . . well, I'm not too sure about the potato salad, it's been around for a while. You'd better just throw it out. There are Ring Dings in the breadbox and ice cream —"

My father sprinted down the front steps carrying his jacket.

"Don't worry, Ma. I know where the food is."

She smiled at me. "I know you know where it is. I just wish you'd look for it more often."

17

"I eat plenty, Ma. I can't help it if I'm built skinny."

"All right, Jeffie, all right. See you later." Almost absentmindedly she tossed the basketball up into the air with one hand and walked down the driveway, not even waiting to see that it swished through the basket without hardly rippling the net.

I waved good-bye to them as they drove away, dribbled the ball a few times, and then went into the house.

Saying that I didn't mind being left alone on a Saturday was not exactly the truth, just as it was not exactly true that I'm not crazy about track meets. If I were one of those kids setting a new record in the high jump, or streaking across the finish line first in the 100-yard dash, and my mother and father were in the stands cheering me on, I think I'd like track meets just fine. But that would be true about anything, I realized.

If there was anything I could do so well that my parents would be proud of me, that *I* would be proud of me, that the kids in school would be impressed by, I'd like it. And if there was something — anything — that I could do with my father on a Saturday afternoon that would make him beam with pride, then sure I'd rather he stay with me and do it, instead of running off to a track meet to watch other kids make their parents cheer.

But there was only one thing I did well, and nobody knew about that except me. And nobody ever would, probably.

I went into my room and got my notebook from my desk drawer. I picked up a pen and started to write.

THE REVENGE OF THE INCREDIBLE DR. RANCID AND HIS YOUTHFUL ASSISTANT, JEFFREY. *Continued*.

Deep in the heart of his hidden mountain laboratory, Dr. Rancid was hard at work on a new formula when Jeffrey, his youthful assistant, pushed the secret button that opened the hidden door on the side of the mountain.

Jeffrey wound his way down the dark maze that led to the laboratory.

Dr. Rancid looked up from the bubbling beaker he was holding.

"So, it is you, Jeffrey. I have been waiting for you. I need your help."

"I thought you might," said Jeffrey. "That's why I'm here."

"We have an enemy, Jeffrey," said Dr. Rancid. "He must be eliminated. His name is —"

"Dewey Belasco," Jeffrey interrupted.

Dr. Rancid looked surprised. "Ah, and now with your many other talents you have taken up mind reading."

"Not really," Jeffrey said modestly. "It's just common knowledge that Dewey Belasco is a menace to almost all mankind and a general pain in the butt."

"True," said Dr. Rancid. "Very true. But he is our *special* enemy, Jeffrey, and that's why it is up to us to do mankind a favor and liquidate him."

19

"I knew he was *my* enemy," said Jeff. "I didn't realize he was your enemy too."

"Any enemy of yours is an enemy of mine," replied Dr. Rancid. "You are valuable to me, Jeff. Very valuable. Belasco knows that. That's why he is after you. Now, I have a plan . . ."

The doorbell rang. I nearly jumped out of my chair. It rang again. Twice.

"*Rats.*" I shoved the notebook into my desk drawer and slammed the door shut. The doorbell rang again as I went down the hall.

"I'm coming!" I yelled. "Keep your shirt on."

I flung open the door without looking out the narrow little window on the side, like my mother always tells me to. It was Mark Winchell, one of the little kids from down the street.

"Is Matthew here?" Matthew is the oldest Winchell kid. He's Bix's age.

"No, Matthew isn't here."

"My mother says to come home for lunch."

"I told you he isn't here," I said impatiently. Then I reminded myself that Mark is only six and how was he supposed to know he was interrupting me?

"Did you try Bix's house?" I asked more gently.

"No." Mark didn't move from the step.

"Well, why don't you try Bix's house?"

"Okay." He still didn't move.

"So long, Mark," I said. Very slowly I started closing the door.

20

"So long." He still wasn't moving. The door clicked shut.

I peeked out the side window. After a moment or two of just standing in front of the closed door, Mark turned and trotted down the steps.

I shook my head and laughed to myself. Mark isn't retarded or anything, he's just what you call a slow mover. His mother says he's a dawdler. She told my mother that Mark is probably a very deep thinker and so spends a lot of time thinking things over before he actually does anything, and no doubt some day he will be very famous for his deep thinking, but in the meantime he's driving her nuts.

Lunch, I remembered. Time to eat. If I didn't make a dent in those cold cuts, my mother would know right away. She probably counts the slices to make sure I've eaten.

Just as I reached the kitchen the phone rang.

"County Morgue," I answered. There was a muffled sound on the other end of the line, then someone — I think a girl — said, "Is this 726-9970?"

"Yeah," I said, beginning to be suspicious.

"Well, this is the telephone repairperson calling. I'll be working on your line for the next hour or so and it's very important that you don't pick up the phone."

"I know —" I began.

"Even if the phone rings," she cut in, "don't pick it up or you'll electrocute me. Remember, whatever you do, don't pick up the phone or I'll be electrocuted."

"I know this joke!" I said, but she had already hung up.

Okay. Fine. It was probably Lana McCabe and her henchpersons with nothing better to do on a Saturday afternoon than hassle Jeff. Why not? Who else?

I spread mustard on my sandwich and bit into it.

The phone rang.

I wouldn't pick it up. I know the joke. They were going to ring and ring until I did. But I wouldn't answer. I didn't have to cooperate in their sadistic little games. Why should I give them the satisfaction?

The phone kept ringing.

What if it isn't Lana? What if they haven't made the second call yet at all? What if it's my mother, trying to get me? An emergency maybe. Or maybe she's worried about me. And the endless ringing of the phone without me here gets her so upset that she leaves the track meet before it's over and rushes home to find out if I'm okay?

But I told them I might be going to the movies.

But it might be *important*. Maybe they were in an accident or something and it's the hospital calling.

The phone kept ringing. The bell seemed to get louder and louder in the empty house.

Maybe it's burglars. Burglars call up places they're planning to rob to see if anyone's home before they try and break in. An unanswered telephone is an invitation to a crook to come on over.

22

And here I am, alone in the house. What if the burglar assumes there's no one home, and breaks in? What if he has a gun? What if he —

The ringing went on and on. I felt like holding my hands over my ears, it seemed so loud. If I didn't answer it, I was going to lose my mind.

I grabbed the receiver off the hook, but held it a short distance from my ear. Sure enough:

"EEEARRGGGHHHH!" came the bloodcurdling scream at the other end of the line.

I could hear the giggles as I slammed the receiver back on the hook.

"I know that joke!" I howled at the phone.

I stormed out of the kitchen, leaving my sandwich, one bite eaten, on the table.

I yanked open my desk drawer and grabbed my notebook. I began to write, pressing the pen so hard into the paper that it made my fingers ache.

Three

"What's that you're reading, Coco?"

Coco Siegelman, my seat partner, looked up from the black-and-white marbled notebook on her desk. Her soft brown eyes met mine for a moment, then looked away quickly.

"It's nothing," she said, closing the book. "Just a silly thing some of the girls are doing."

Mr. Burkett was writing on the chalkboard.

"What kind of a silly thing?"

"It's a slam book," she said softly.

Everything about Coco is soft. Her eyes, her voice, her honey-colored hair . . . she even wears soft clothes. Some people, like Lana McCabe, for instance, are all hard angles and sharp edges, but Coco . . . well, enough about Coco. She's just a nice person who never says a mean thing about anyone, including me.

"What's a slam book?"

"It's really so *silly*. You just write down what you think of people in it."

"What people?"

"People you know."

"Let me see it," I said.

She put her arm over the book. "Oh, Jeff, just the girls are doing it. The boys aren't supposed to see it."

I pulled the notebook out from under her hand and opened it. The pages were folded closed, and there was a name written on each page.

I opened Dewey Belasco's page. On each line of the page there was a comment about Dewey. They were all in different handwritings:

An ape a day keeps the doctor away.

The incredible hulk lives!

Class Clod.

Big and strong. The person who wrote that had dotted the *i* in *big* with a little circle.

Phooey on Dewey.

I think he's cute but I'd be afraid to let him hug me.

I think so too and I'm not afraid.

I shook my head.

"I told you it was silly," Coco whispered.

I flipped the pages and came to one with my name on it. It practically leaped out of the book at me. *Jeffrey Childs.* The *i* in *Childs* was dotted with a circle.

I was almost tempted to give the slam book back

to Coco without looking at what they had written about me. I had a sickening feeling I wouldn't like what I read.

But I couldn't do it. My curiosity was too strong, and I was too weak to just close the book and pretend not to care what people thought about me.

Slowly, carefully, almost like I could be burnt by the paper, I unfolded the page with my name on it.

Scared of his own shadow.

He's too thin to have *a shadow.*

Childish lives down to his name.

Skinny chicken. The *i*'s in both words were dotted with circles.

Smart and nice. I couldn't believe that one. I read it over three times. I glanced at Coco. Could she have written it? She had her head down and seemed to be concentrating very hard on rubbing ballpoint ink off one of her fingers.

If he *hugged you, you wouldn't feel it.*

Why would you let *him hug you? Ugh!*

My stomach turned over. I felt my throat tighten as I folded down my page and closed the book. I shoved it onto Coco's desk.

Mr. Burkett turned around from the chalkboard.

"Isn't it dumb?" Coco whispered.

I swallowed hard. "Yeah," I muttered. I felt like I could hardly choke the words out. "Very dumb."

Coco dropped the book over her shoulder to Shirley Matson, who sat in the desk behind her. Mr. Burkett was talking now, probably about the stuff he'd written on the chalkboard, but I wasn't hearing him.

It's one thing to know that people don't like you. It's another thing to see how much they don't like you written down in a notebook for anybody to read. Every girl in the class was going to see those things written about me. You might as well print them in the newspaper with a big headline: ALMOST EVERYONE AGREES JEFFREY CHILDS IS A CREEP.

And to know that not only don't they like me (which I already knew anyhow) but that they think I'm *disgusting* — I mean, I don't have the slightest urge to hug any girl in the class, and that's the truth — almost the truth, anyway — but it's a killer to know that if I *did* hug someone she'd throw up.

My face felt clammy, and for a moment I had a horrible feeling that *I* would throw up, right in the middle of the class. That's all I needed. That's all *they* needed.

I closed my eyes and concentrated hard on not throwing up.

Mr. Burkett stopped talking and I heard the chalk clicking on the board again.

"You should see what they wrote about other people," Coco whispered, her lips right next to my ear.

My eyes flew open.

"They're just trying to be smart alecks," she said. "That's all. Everyone's trying to be witty."

I managed a weak nod. Sure. Witty.

28

"They wrote all kinds of mean things about Danny Frankel."

She was trying to make me feel better, but she was just making me feel worse. She wouldn't be trying to cheer me up if she didn't see how much that stupid slam book bothered me, and I didn't want her to know how much it *did* bother me. But I was doing a rotten job of hiding my feelings, or else she wouldn't have kept on about it.

Besides, Danny Frankel happens to be a perfectly okay kid, and since nobody ever said nasty things to his face, I wasn't sure I believed anyone would write nasty things about him for other people to read.

Of course, no one ever said nasty things about Dewey Belasco either, but that was because they were afraid of immediate death if they did.

At lunchtime I usually looked for where Dewey was sitting and then found the farthest table from his that had an empty seat. I slumped a lot in the lunchroom, trying to make myself as inconspicuous as possible so Dewey wouldn't notice me and come over to start something.

He hardly ever does in the lunchroom, probably because he won't let anything, not even his pleasure in hounding me, interfere with cramming everything in sight into his mouth. He'd probably wolf down the tray, too, if they didn't make us hand them back.

After lunch, if he didn't spot me, I could usually avoid him by staying in when he went out, or going out when he stayed in. He usually went out, so I usually stayed in. What he did for fun without me around I'm not sure, but I always suspected he looked for the nearest tree and hung from it, scratching under his arms occasionally.

Today I found a seat next to Danny Frankel and Ray Krusinski.

"Hey, Jeff," Danny greeted me.

"Hey, Danny." I slid in next to him.

"Childs," said Ray, "did you buy or bring?"

Since I had just put down my tray, I thought it was pretty obvious that I had bought lunch today, but I didn't want to be unfriendly. I couldn't afford to be unfriendly. Ray isn't a problem, though he looks tough. I couldn't call him my friend — well, I couldn't exactly call anyone my friend, except Bix — but at least he wasn't an enemy.

"I bought."

Ray snorted. "Some guys never learn. You eat enough of this food, it'll kill ya." He opened a brown paper bag.

Two tables over from us, Lana McCabe and a couple of her friends were huddled together. Every once in a while, a burst of giggles erupted from their direction. I didn't even have to take a second to wonder what they were laughing about.

"What's with them?" asked Ray.

Danny shrugged. "Some notebook, that's all I saw."

"Yeah? Why should they have fits over a notebook?"

30

"Maybe it has dirty pictures in it," I said, trying to make a joke. The last thing I wanted was for any more people to see that notebook than already had.

But what a dumb thing to say if I wanted Ray to forget about the slam book! His eyes lit up like candle flames.

"You think so? You think that's it?"

Danny laughed. "Stop drooling, Ray. Jeff was only kidding."

"Were you kidding? You don't think there are really dirty pictures in there?" The gleam faded from Ray's eyes.

"Only kidding," I nodded. "Really, Ray, just my little joke."

"But we don't *know*," Ray said. He started to look all eager again. "We don't know what's in that book. We could get it and find out."

No! Coco had said only the girls were doing it. That meant only the girls were *reading* it. At least only half the class would know all the rotten things people had written about me. And only the girl half. But if Ray got hold of it — if he passed it around — if everyone saw it, all the guys too — if Dewey Belasco saw it —

I groaned to myself and pushed away my lunch tray. I wasn't going to be able to eat now.

"But, um, how are you going to get it, Ray?" I asked, trying to sound very uninterested.

Ray gave me a puzzled stare, like he didn't understand me at all.

"I'll just go over there and take it, that's all."

31

"Oh. Yeah. Sure." How else?

"Aw, forget it, Ray. What do you care what they're doing?" Danny said. "Those girls would laugh at a muscular dystrophy telethon."

"Right," I added hastily. "And besides, they're probably just waiting for someone to come over and see what they're doing. Why give them the satisfaction?"

Ray looked blank. "The satisfaction of what?"

I tried not to be impatient with him. "The satisfaction of falling for it."

Ray thought that over for a moment. "Well, I don't care," he said stubbornly. "I'm going to see what it is. You guys coming with me?"

What little lunch I'd eaten began to turn over in my stomach.

Were us guys coming with him? I looked over at Danny. He was munching contentedly on a sandwich.

"I'm still eating, Ray," he said.

Ray looked at me pointedly.

I yanked my lunch tray back in front of me and dug a fork into the chow mein. "I'm still eating too," I said, almost apologetically. I wanted it to sound like if I didn't have to finish this lunch, I would be the first to leap up and join him in the raid on Lana McCabe's table.

"Well, I'm going." Ray hauled himself up from the bench. I put down my forkful of chow mein. I couldn't even look at the stuff, let alone push any of it past my lips.

32

I craned my head around to watch Ray. He walked over to Lana's table and simply reached over her for the book, which the girl next to her was holding.

There was a loud squeal, then a series of squeals and shrieks, and Lana jumped up from the table and hurled an apple at Ray's head. Ray ducked and the apple hit a dish of chow mein on the table behind him.

The kid whose chow mein had been bombed let out an angry howl and leaped up, chow mein dripping down his shirt front.

Ray still hadn't gotten the book, I saw with relief. It was, I realized, the only time in my life I would ever root for Lana McCabe.

Ray lunged for the book, which was now being passed from girl to girl down the table. Every time he made a swipe for it, another girl had it. All the girls at the table were screaming at him now. The kid with the chow mein down his front chucked a carton of milk at Lana. As the container hit the table and milk poured all over, sloshing onto the laps of several girls, a lunchroom aide charged into the middle of the action, arms waving wildly.

"WHAT IS GOING ON HERE?" Without waiting for an answer, she grabbed Ray by the arm, and the kid with the chow mein shirt by his arm. Ray just stood there, sullenly, but the kid who'd gotten splattered was yelling at the top of his lungs. "She threw an apple at me! Look what she did to me!"

Meanwhile, half the girls at Lana's table (including, I was delighted to note, Lana) had jumped up and were hopping around and making disgusted "ooh" and "ugh" sounds about the milk soaking their clothes.

"OUT!" the aide ordered, propelling Ray and the other kid toward the door.

"But she started it! Look at my shirt!" The kid never stopped howling all the way out the door.

"Ohh!" Shirley Matson groaned. "Look, it got all wet." She was holding the notebook. I wanted to cheer.

"It'll dry," said Lana, wringing out her skirt.

"No, look, all the pages are clumping together. It's ruined," Barbara Boyle wailed.

Hooray! I thought. Hallelujah! Good old Ray!

"That's okay," said Lana, her voice hard. "We'll just make another one."

I gave one short, strangled little cry and put my head in my hands. Danny didn't even notice. He was thoughtfully drilling into the center of a jelly doughnut with his tongue.

"Hey, Childish, c'mere! Lemme sneeze on you!"

I kept my head down and walked faster.

"Hey, whatsa matter, Childish? Why you running from me?"

I wasn't running. I was just walking very fast. Bix had to trot to keep up with me.

"Aw, c'mon, Childish. I just wanna see if it's true that you'll blow away if I sneeze on you."

I clenched my teeth. Ignoring him was not

working, but nothing would work with Dewey. Unless I was bigger than he was. But if I was, he wouldn't be doing this.

"Don't let him get away with that stuff, Jeffie," Bix panted. "Tell him off."

"You tell him off," I said sarcastically.

Bix whirled around to face Dewey, who was several feet behind us.

"I was only kidding, Bix!" I hissed frantically. But it was too late.

"You better stop!" Bix yelled. "You just better stop that!"

I grabbed Bix by the shoulder. "Are you crazy?"

"You can't talk to my friend that way!"

"BIX!" I yanked at his arm.

Dewey stopped in his tracks. He began to laugh. He was laughing so hard that when I turned to look back he was doubled over, clutching his stomach.

"That your bodyguard, Childish?" he roared after us. "Boy, is he tough! Ooh, I'm scared to death!"

My face was flaming as I dragged Bix along till there was plenty of distance between Dewey and me. Bix had distracted him enough to let us get away before anything further happened, but if I was supposed to be grateful, I wasn't. I was humiliated. How many people had seen an eight-year-old kid threaten Dewey while I ran the other way? I don't know, since I'd been staring at the ground while I was running — I mean, walking extremely fast.

I turned around to look back once more and saw Coco Siegelman coming toward us.

"Ohh," I groaned softly.

"What's the matter, Jeffie? I got him to stop, didn't I?"

"Don't ever do that again, Bix. *Ever*."

"But that's what friends are for, right? Friends are supposed to stick up for each other." Bix sounded insulted.

How could I tell him that he'd just made everything worse? How could I explain that he'd gotten Dewey off my back for one afternoon, by taking him by surprise, but that he'd given him even more ammunition for his next attack?

"Just let me handle this my own way," I said as we reached our block.

"But you're not handling it," Bix pointed out.

"Yeah, well, that's part of my strategy."

"What strategy?" Bix asked curiously.

Good question.

THE REVENGE OF THE INCREDIBLE DR. RANCID AND HIS YOUTHFUL ASSISTANT, JEFFREY. *Continued*.

When Jeffrey, armed with Dr. Rancid's powerful new invention, the Stun Gun, reached the abandoned shack in the woods where Dewey Belasco and his evil assistant, Lana, were holed up, he heard several female screams.

"Oh, oh, help, help! Please help me!"

What horrible thing was going on in that shack? Jeffrey's blood ran cold as he thought of the helpless victim they must have in there.

He crept up to a window and peeked in. To his

shock, he saw Coco Siegelman tied to a chair. It was her who had been screaming. Dewey Belasco stood over her, smiling an ugly, evil smile.

"Help, oh, please, help me, somebody!" Coco cried.

"No one's gonna hear you," Dewey said gruffly. "Go ahead and scream all you want."

I must save her, thought Jeffrey. Dewey Belasco is capable of *anything*. I must save her before it's Too Late.

But where was Dewey's cunning and cruel assistant, Lana McCabe? Jeffrey's eyes scanned the inside of the little shack, quickly taking in everything there was to see. Lana was nowhere to be seen.

He had to make his move now. Even if Lana was there, in another room or out back or something, there was no telling what Dewey would do to Coco if Jeff waited any longer. There was no time to lose.

Jeffrey sneaked around to the door of the shack and hurled himself against it.

The door crashed open and Dewey spun around in surprise.

"You!" he gasped. He charged toward Jeffrey like an angry bull, and Jeffrey pulled the trigger of the Stun Gun. Dewey froze, his face still in a horrible scowl. He would stay frozen that way for at least two hours.

"Oh, Jeffie, thank goodness!" cried Coco. "He was going to —"

Suddenly there was a loud shriek of anger. Lana McCabe came leaping through the shattered window on the side of the cabin. Jeffrey whirled around and, with perfect aim, zapped her with the Stun Gun. Lana was caught in midair and frozen in space right in the middle of her jump.

"Oh, Jeffie, you saved me! You saved me!" Coco started to cry softly.

Jeffrey tucked the Stun Gun into his belt and reached down to free Coco from her ropes.

"Keep calm, Coco," he said. "I have everything under control."

Coco jumped up as soon as she was untied. Her face was white with shock. "Oh, Jeffie, you were just in time! I think . . . I think he wanted to *kiss* me."

He was probably thinking of worse things than that, Jeffrey knew, but there was no point in getting Coco any more upset than she already was.

"Try not to think about it," he said. "I'm here now. I'll take care of you."

"Just imagine, Jeffie — Dewey *kissing* me! Oh, ugh!"

"Ugh's the word all right." Jeffrey put his arm around her shoulders reassuringly. "And listen, kid —," his voice was gruff but kind — "don't call me Jeffie."

Four

In movies and on TV, when a kid is being bullied, his father teaches him how to box. "Now," his father says, after he's taught the kid all the moves, "now you can defend yourself." And the kid stands up to the bully at last, and after taking a few punches, decks the bully with a good clip to the nose and is never bothered again.

Real life is a lot more complicated than movies and TV. First of all, if I asked my father to teach me to box, he'd want to know why. Then the whole story about Dewey would come out and he'd know what a coward I was. I wanted him to be proud of me, not to pity me.

Second of all, I don't think my father knows *how* to box. (Though my mother probably does.) Third of all, in real life, guys like Dewey Belasco don't pay much attention to the rules of boxing laid down by the Federal Boxing Commission, or whoever it is who makes the rules. If I were to raise my fists toward Dewey's face and say, "Put up your dukes and fight like a man," he'd probably grab me around the throat, lift me off the ground like a skinny chicken, wring my neck for a few minutes, and then toss me against a brick wall.

The phone rang.

"Oh, Jeffie, thank goodness you're home!"

"Mrs. Winchell?" Mrs. Winchell is Matthew, Mark, and Fletcher's mother.

"Listen, Jeff, this is an emergency. My husband won't be in till six and our regular baby-sitter has a stomach virus and no one in the world seems to be home and I have my midterm abnormal psychology exam in *half an hour* —"

"You want me to stay with the kids?"

"Oh, please, Jeffie, if you can. I'll pay you — I should have left by now —"

"No problem. I'll be right over. And you don't have to pay me."

"We'll talk about that later. Just *come!*"

"On my way."

I hung up the phone, grabbed my jacket from the closet, and ran out the front door and down the steps. It was four o'clock and my mother had left a note saying she'd be late and we'd go out to eat when she got home.

It was raining lightly when I got to the Winchell's house down the block, and Mrs. Winchell was standing at the door, holding it open for me.

40

"You're a lifesaver, honey," she said. "I'll only be two hours, but Dave should be home first and you can leave when he gets here." Dave is her husband.

"Don't worry about it," I said. She really looked frantic. She often does, but not usually this frantic.

Mrs. Winchell is going to college, and between her three kids and classes and the house, she's probably got her hands full.

"Don't worry about a thing," I said. "Good luck on your exam."

"Thanks, dear." She patted the air near my head — I think she meant to pat me on the head, but she was in a hurry. She waved to Matthew, Mark, and Fletcher, who were lined up in the hall behind her. "Be good for Jeff, now, boys." She ran out the door.

I'd never actually baby-sat for the Winchell kids before, but I played with them and Bix occasionally so I really didn't think there'd be any problems. They're good kids and young enough to look up to me as one of the "big kids."

Matthew is eight, Mark is six, and Fletcher is four. They look a lot alike, all with straight blond hair and blue eyes. Standing there lined up in size place, they were really sort of cute.

I herded them into the family room and we sat down in a circle on the floor.

"Okay, men," I said briskly, "what'll we do? Who wants to watch TV?"

"ME!" yelled Fletcher, as if he hardly ever got the chance to watch TV.

"Let's play basketball," Matthew said.

"No, it's raining out. It's no good playing in the rain."

"I want to play Uncle Wiggily," said Mark.

"Isn't there something you all like to do?" I asked.

They looked at each other thoughtfully. Matthew's eyes lit up.

"Yeah! Make concoctions."

"Yeah! Coctions!" Fletcher yelled.

Mark nodded. "We all like that."

"What's making concoctions?" I asked.

Matthew smiled happily. "We go into the bathroom and mix up a whole lot of things from the medicine cabinet and add some food coloring or paint or something and maybe some soap so it bubbles."

"Then what do you do with it?" I asked nervously.

Matthew shrugged. "Usually flush it down the toilet. Unless we wanted to kill somebody. Then we'd try to get him to drink it."

"I don't think your mother would like that too much."

"That's why we should do it now," Matthew said.

Very logical.

"No concoctions," I said sternly. "Now, what else do you all like to do?"

"Watch 'The Flintstones'!" yelled Fletcher.

"Play Uncle Wiggily," Mark insisted.

"Make a cake," said Matthew.

That didn't sound like a bad idea. If Mrs. Winchell had any cake mix around it should be pretty easy, and think how pleased she'd be when she came back to find a nice, homemade cake waiting for her.

"I'll tell you what. We'll mix up the cake and then, while it's baking, we'll play Uncle Wiggily. How's that, Mark?"

Mark thought about it for a minute. "Okay."

"Come on, Fletcher. We're going to make a cake and then play Uncle Wiggily."

"Don't know how to make a cake," said Fletcher. He turned on the television and plopped down on his huge stuffed turtle in front of the screen.

" 'The Flintstones'!" he yelled. " 'The Flintstones' is on!" He bounced up and down on his turtle.

"Oh, let him watch," Matthew said. "He'd just be in the way anyhow."

"Okay, you watch 'The Flintstones,' but *don't move*. Okay, Fletcher?"

Fletcher was staring at the set. He didn't look like he'd ever move.

"Don't worry," said Matthew. "He'd stay there all night if you let him."

We went into the kitchen and Matthew found a box of cake mix. He got out a bowl and the eggs. The electric mixer was right on the counter, and both Matthew and Mark insisted they knew how to use it.

They each got to break one egg into the bowl.

We were picking eggshells out of the cake mix

when there was a horrible scream from the family room.

I raced in there and found Fletcher holding his mouth and crying.

"Fletcher, what happened?" I grabbed his hand away from his mouth. I thought my heart was going to stop. He was bleeding like a stuck pig. Blood seemed to be gushing out of his mouth, down his chin.

"Oh, my God! Fletcher, what happened? What did you do?" He just kept screaming and crying.

I was panic-stricken. How much could a little kid like that bleed before he lost too much blood? And how had he hurt himself so badly? And what was I going to do? My mother wasn't home, and Mrs. Winchell said *nobody* was home —

"Matthew," I said, trying to sound calm, except that my voice was shaking, "get me one of your father's clean handkerchiefs."

Matthew ran upstairs and was back down again in a minute with a handkerchief. I tried to press it against Fletcher's lip, but he twisted around and screamed right through the handkerchief.

"It's okay, Fletcher," I said. "It's okay. This'll make it better."

But it didn't. He seemed to bleed even more.

I picked him up. I remembered that three blocks away, on Staunton Road, there was a house with a doctor's name sign on the front. We don't go to him but it was close and at the moment, that was the only thing I could think of to do.

"You two, get your raincoats and umbrellas if you have them. Hurry up, we're taking Fletcher to the doctor."

"What doctor?" asked Mark.

"MOVE IT!" I yelled. "Get Fletcher's coat too."

They ran. Even Mark didn't dawdle.

My heart pounding, I carried Fletcher into the kitchen. I washed off the handkerchief and put it against his lips again. He was only crying now, not screaming anymore.

There was a blackboard in the kitchen with *Yogurt, milk, coffee, granola*, written on it. I wrote under that, *I took Fletcher to the doctor. Don't worry. Jeff*. If Mr. or Mrs. Winchell got back before we did and saw the blood on the floor in the family room and kitchen, at least they'd know I had the situation under control.

Sure I did. I was shaking so hard I could have homogenized Fletcher.

Matthew and Mark were back in an instant. We put Fletcher's coat and hat on and ran down the front steps.

It was raining much harder now. "You guys walk under the umbrella," I said, "and let's go."

We jogged the three blocks to the doctor's. Fletcher is not a particularly heavy kid, but neither am I, so by the time we reached the door my arms were aching. I rang the bell and walked in.

The waiting room was full of people. I staggered up to the nurse at the desk and gasped, "Emergency. *Please*." She looked at the four of us. Mark was

45

holding the open umbrella and dripping all over the carpet.

"What kind of emergency?"

I held out the bloody handkerchief for her to see.

"All right, take a seat please. I'll have the doctor see him right away."

We didn't take a seat. We just stood there. She went somewhere down a hall and came back a few minutes later.

"Come with me, please." I followed her, and Matthew and Mark followed me.

"You boys," she said, "wait out there, all right?"

"He's my brother," Matthew said.

"Don't worry. We'll take good care of him. Just wait in the reception room."

"Go on," I told Matthew. "You watch Mark."

I carried Fletcher down the hall. The nurse led me into a small room with an examining table. "Just put him down there," she said.

Fletcher looked around. He must have finally realized he was in a doctor's office, because he began to wail.

"No shots! No shots!" The bleeding didn't look so bad now, but his chin and mouth were a mess of red smears.

A real tall guy in a white coat came into the room. Except for the white coat, he looked more like a football player than a doctor.

"Is this the patient?" he asked pleasantly, putting his hand on Fletcher's head.

"No shots!" yelled Fletcher. "No shots!"

46

"Well." The doctor smiled. "He sounds in pretty good shape."

"This really was an emergency," I said. I didn't want the doctor to think I shouldn't have bothered him. "I was baby-sitting with him and all of a sudden he yelled and he was bleeding all over the rug. His mouth."

"Yes. Open your mouth, son."

"No shots!" Fletcher yelled. The doctor ducked his head down and grabbed a peek at Fletcher's mouth.

"What happened to him?"

"I don't know," I said miserably. "We were making a cake. He was in the other room watching television. I shouldn't have left him alone."

"Let's get this cleaned up and take a look. Why don't you wait outside?"

"He's just a little kid. He'll be scared."

The door opened and another nurse walked in.

"Not with Jeannie here," the doctor said. He looked at Fletcher. "You're not scared, are you?" Fletcher looked at Jeannie.

Jeannie smiled. "And what's *your* name?"

"No shots," Fletcher said, but more quietly now.

"What a nice name, No Shots. What's your last name, No Shots?"

Fletcher giggled.

I was so relieved, I left him there with the doctor and Jeannie and went into the waiting room.

Matthew and Mark were sitting in the middle of the reception-room floor, their slickers still dripping little puddles around them. The umbrella was open and Mark was twirling it upside down in front of him, like a top.

"He'll be okay," I said. "The doctor's taking care of him. Close the umbrella, Mark."

"I don't know how."

Matthew reached for it and closed it. "Did they find out why he was bleeding like that?"

I shook my head. "No, but the doctor'll take care of him."

I slumped down into a chair and tried not to show the boys how upset I was. I didn't know what the doctor would have to do to Fletcher, but whatever it was, I knew it was my fault for leaving him alone. How would I ever explain this to Mrs. Winchell?

The nurse at the desk called me over. "I'll need some information about him. He's not a patient of ours, is he?"

"I don't think so. I'm his baby-sitter. Those are his brothers."

Some baby-sitter, I thought. She was probably thinking the same thing.

I gave Fletcher's name and age, and Matthew gave the nurse his parents' names and their address and telephone number.

"Do you have any relatives in the vicinity?" she asked Matthew. He looked at her blankly.

"Does any of your family live around here?" I asked him.

"My mother and father," he said.

"Besides them."

He shook his head.

48

I began to get even more worried. "You mean, next of kin?" Why did they need to know the next of kin? That was what you had to know when someone was *dying*.

"Is it that serious?" I tried to keep my voice down so as not to worry the kids, but my heart began to pound like a hammer. I thought I would keel over before she said, "Of course not. We just like to know if there's an adult relative to sign forms and things if necessary."

"Why would it be necessary?" My voice shook.

But before she could answer, Fletcher came trotting down the hall, one hand in Jeannie's, proudly waving a wooden tongue depressor.

"He's fine!" the nurse said. "And he was *so* brave. Weren't you brave, No Shots?"

Fletcher laughed delightedly.

"The doctor wants to see you for a minute." She pointed down the hall.

I practically ran down the hall and found the doctor washing up in the little room where Fletcher had been.

"What happened?" I asked breathlessly. "What did you have to do? Is he okay?"

"He's fine. All it was, really, was a cut upper lip. It looked a lot worse than it was. You know, those mouth and lip cuts bleed like crazy. They scare the heck out of most parents."

I breathed a loud sigh of relief and slumped against the wall. "He doesn't need stitches or anything?"

"I don't think so. I didn't want to do anything too

much without his parents here. The bleeding is stopped, so it ought to be okay."

"Did you find out how it happened?"

"The nearest I could figure out," the doctor said, drying his hands, "is that he got into a fight with a turtle."

"Ohh. He must have been wrestling with his stuffed turtle."

"Then he probably just bit his lip hard. But since we don't know for sure, tell his parents to call me. If he's not up to date on his shots, his own doctor should give him a tetanus shot. You be sure and have them call me when they get home, all right?"

"All right," I said. "Thanks a lot."

I went back into the waiting room. Fletcher was standing on a chair, waving his tongue depressor around like a symphony conductor.

"Let's go, guys. Come on, Fletcher, we'll get your coat and hat on."

"No Shots," said Fletcher. He jumped up and down on the chair. "Name is No Shots."

I grabbed him and got his coat on. "No jumping, No Shots. No jumping, no running, no turtle wrestling."

Three people in the waiting room tittered.

Very funny.

It wasn't until we trudged back to the Winchell's house that I realized that I had no key and we'd locked ourselves out. So we went to my house and Matthew kept watch at the front window till he saw his father's car pull into their driveway.

My stomach jerked crazily. I was not looking forward to explaining this.

I got Fletcher's slicker back on, and we went down the block to the Winchells'. Mr. Winchell had just opened the front door when we reached the house.

"Hey, what's up, kids? What are you doing out in this rain?"

Fletcher waved his tongue depressor as he trotted into the house. "My turtle bit me and I was bleeding and the doctor gave me this because I was so brave."

"*What?*"

My heart sinking into my stomach, I explained.

Mr. Winchell looked stunned for a moment. Then he bent down in front of Fletcher. "Let's see where your turtle bit you."

Fletcher opened his mouth.

"Oh, that doesn't look so bad," he said.

"It was bad," said Fletcher. "It was *very* bad. I was *bleeding*. It *hurt*. Is 'The Flintstones' on?" Still wearing his raincoat, he wandered off into the family room.

"I'm really sorry, Mr. Winchell. I left him alone in there and I shouldn't have. It's all my fault."

"Jeff, I'm very grateful you were here. You can't watch him every minute. Good grief, he's in there alone half the day. This could have happened anytime. You were terrific, the way you handled the whole thing. You should be very proud of yourself."

I shook my head. I think he was just being nice.

There wouldn't have been anything to handle if I had kept my eye on Fletcher.

I gave him the doctor's card, which the nurse had given me before we left the office.

"I'd better go call him. Listen, Jeff, thanks a million. Thanks for *everything*."

"Sure. So long, Matthew. So long, Mark."

"Bye, Jeff," said Matthew. Mark didn't say anything for a minute. Then, as I was halfway out the door, he called, "Jeff? You promised to play Uncle Wiggily."

I was still feeling pretty upset when my parents got home, and even dinner out at Cliff's Shore Manor didn't do a thing to make me feel better.

My parents kept asking me why I was in such a bad mood, but I didn't want to tell them. I was somehow hoping they'd never find out about the whole thing. I could imagine how proud of me they'd be if they knew that while I was supposed to be responsible for the Winchell kids I had let one of them practically bleed to death.

A few minutes after we got back from the restaurant, the doorbell rang.

My father went to open it and there was Mrs. Winchell, her hair damp and frizzing, not even wearing a raincoat. She was breathless.

"Oh, Jeff!" She headed right for me. "Liz, Spence, did you hear what happened? Did you hear what Jeff did?"

I wanted to shrink into the walls before she could grab me — I thought she might want to clout me a good one in the head. I was stunned when she grabbed me and hugged me so hard I couldn't breathe for a minute.

Then she told them the whole thing — very dramatically.

"Jeff, you were just — just —" She grabbed me and hugged me again. "You should be proud of this boy," she said to my mother. "He saved the day. I don't know what would have happened if he wasn't there."

I was getting more and more embarrassed by the minute. When she pressed some bills into my hand, I cringed.

"*No!*" I tried to hand them back but she wouldn't take them.

"Please, Mrs. Winchell, I don't want any money. I'm just sorry that Fletcher got hurt when I was supposed to be watching him."

"Are you crazy, Jeffie? He gets hurt while *I'm* watching him. If I felt guilty every time one of those three got a cut or a bruise, I'd be in a rubber room by now. And you keep that money. It's not nearly enough for what you did. You just better know how grateful we are, that's all."

My parents were standing there looking dazed as she let herself out the front door.

"Why didn't you tell us?"

"Jeff, I'm so proud of you," my mother said.

"You really come through in an emergency." My father was beaming at me, as if I had won the 100-yard dash, or something.

What was the matter with everybody? Why

couldn't they see what I saw? I had loused things up again, and everyone was praising me like I was some kind of hero or something.

I stuffed the money Mrs. Winchell had forced on me into a pocket. "It was my fault in the first place," I muttered. "Nothing to be proud of."

But they kept beaming at me and carrying on about it for the whole rest of the evening, so that by the time I went to bed, I was beginning to let myself feel just the tiniest little bit like a hero.

Five

Bix was waiting on the front steps in the morning.

"Hey, Jeff, I heard you saved Fletcher's life!"

Boy, Mrs. Winchell gets around.

"I didn't actually save his life, Bix. I just took him to the doctor, that's all."

"Yeah, but Mrs. Winchell told my mother he was practically bleeding to death and you knew just what to do."

"Aw, it was really nothing, Bix."

I felt pretty good this morning. What with the Winchells' being so grateful, and my parents getting so worked up over the whole thing that they couldn't talk about anything else the whole night, I figured that if all those people thought I was the nearest thing to a hero, well, maybe they were right and I was wrong. After all, they're older than I am.

"I'd know what to do too," said Bix.

"Yeah?" I smiled. Maybe Bix was a little jealous of the fuss everyone was making over me.

"Sure. I'd just look it up in my first-aid cards. They tell you what to do for anything — snakebite, twisted ankle, beestings, broken arms —"

"Well, next time there's an accident I'll call you."

"Okay." Bix looked pleased at the idea. I had this funny feeling he was eager for me to get some sort of crippling injury so I could call him to look it up in his first-aid cards.

Bix peppered me with questions about Fletcher's accident all the way to school and I told him the whole story, just like it happened. I only left out the parts about how scared I was and how miserable I'd felt about letting Fletcher get hurt, because by now I was feeling so good about myself that I really believed what everybody else seemed to believe. Bix's "oh's" and "ah's" of admiration didn't do a thing to spoil my mood either.

By the time we got to school I was feeling about six feet tall and husky as a fullback. I didn't look for Dewey as I went upstairs to the classroom. I didn't even think about him as I went into the room and right to my desk.

I sat down next to Coco and flashed her a big grin. "Hey, Coco."

"Hey, Jeff," she said softly.

Suddenly I remembered how she'd been tied up

in the abandoned shack and how I'd rescued her and how grateful she'd been . . . and my face started getting hot, almost like I had a fever.

What if she knew what I was thinking? What if she ever saw my notebook? Maybe she was the one who wrote in the slam book that she'd like Dewey to hug her. Maybe she was the one who wrote, "Why would you let *him* hug you? *Ugh!*" about me. Would she, in real life, get nauseous if I put my arm around her the way I had in my story? Maybe she wouldn't want me to rescue her from Dewey.

My face got hotter and hotter. What was the matter with me? I turned my head so that if I was blushing Coco couldn't see it. I had to stop thinking these things. I didn't know if I was blushing, but I ordered myself not to. I concentrated very hard on not blushing. Slowly my face returned to its normal temperature.

After the Pledge of Allegiance, Mr. Burkett said, "Today we have a very special treat. The Burnham County Drugmobile is going to be here all day and the sixth grades are going to go through it."

"Yay," said Arnie Kopell, "they're giving away drugs."

"Very funny, Arnie."

Going through a Drugmobile is not my idea of a very special treat, but then again, it beats taking a spelling test.

"This will be an educational experience. It's very interesting, I promise you. I've seen it myself already and you'll have a chance to ask the narcotics squad officer all the questions you can think of about drug abuse."

Arnie waved his hand in the air. "Mr. Burkett, Mr. Burkett!"

Mr. Burkett looked suspicious. "Yes, Arnie?"

"In health they told us that alcohol abuse was a bigger problem among kids now than drugs. So how come they don't have a boozemobile?"

Some of the kids laughed. Mr. Burkett looked thoughtful.

"That's a good question to ask the officer. Why don't you keep it in mind when you go through the Drugmobile?"

We went downstairs and into the school yard, where the Drugmobile was parked. It was a long, white van. It looked like a mobile home without windows. It had a door on the side and a little set of steps up to the door. BURNHAM COUNTY DRUGMOBILE was painted in blue letters on the side.

We lined up in front of the steps and Mr. Burkett led us in, single file. Coco was in front of me and — I don't know how it happened, except that I wasn't alert for it — Dewey Belasco was right behind me.

One whole side of the van was set up with pictures and displays of drug stuff. A man in a plain blue suit introduced himself as Detective Sheaff of the narcotics squad.

"I'm going to explain all these different items to you and if you have any questions feel free to ask them. We want you kids to be aware of the dangers

58

of drugs, and the Drugmobile is one of the ways we try to educate you."

"I have a question," said Dewey. "Can we call you Nark?"

The detective gave a weak little smile. He must have heard that one a thousand times. "*Detective* Nark, if you don't mind."

Everybody laughed except Dewey. I started to laugh, but thought better of it. I cleared my throat instead.

"Now the first display we have here is marijuana. A lot of you have probably never seen what marijuana actually looks like. I hope you haven't. We put marijuana first in our display because usually it's the first drug kids try. There are a lot of different names for marijuana. It's called 'pot,' 'grass,' 'maryjane,' . . ." On and on went the list of names. It was like a vocabulary lesson. If I'm ever on a quiz show and they ask me ten different slang words for marijuana, I'm ready.

Then he showed us cigarette papers and a rolling machine, and gave us a whole list of names for what marijuana cigarettes are called ("reefers," "joints," etc.).

By the time we got to cocaine, the whole thing was beginning to sound like a "how-to" lesson. Detective Sheaff told us how each drug was taken: smoked, sniffed, injected, whatever, and what it did to your body.

We got to see amphetamines, angel dust, heroin — you name it, we learned about it.

59

Dewey asked if they were giving away free samples.

Detective Sheaff smiled again. That was another one he'd heard a thousand times, I'll bet.

Then Detective Sheaff told us about the penalties for being caught using or selling drugs. Not only would we probably kill ourselves and/or ruin our lives if we touched any of this stuff, but if we somehow managed to survive taking the drugs, the cops would definitely catch us and we'd spend a few years to life in jail.

The whole thing got pretty boring after a while. I had heard most of this stuff before, and even though I hadn't actually seen little envelopes of heroin and little packets of cocaine, I had never particularly wanted to, either.

Barbara Boyle asked how you could tell the difference between cocaine and heroin, and Arnie Kopell said yeah, you didn't want to sniff what you were supposed to shoot up.

Mr. Burkett asked Arnie if he remembered the *intelligent* question he'd meant to ask the detective and Arnie didn't.

"About a boozemobile," Lana said. She giggled. She even giggles nasty.

Detective Sheaff explained that they were now combining narcotics and alcohol abuse into one unit and soon they would fix up a van with information on both.

"When it's ready," he said, "we'll come back for another visit, if you like, and you can learn about alcohol abuse."

I could wait. I know what liquor looks like.

I was glad when the talk was over and Detective Sheaff told us to take some of the pamphlets laid out on a little table. As I had already learned more about drugs than I'd ever wanted to know, I passed up the pamphlets and started toward the door of the Drugmobile, following Coco.

Dewey tapped me on the shoulder. His finger was about as gentle as a falling tree trunk.

"Hey, Childish, don't you want to know more about cocaine?" His feet scraped the back of my heels as I went down the steps. I nearly walked out of my sneakers.

"I thought you liked cocaine, Childish."

Half the class was already milling around outside the Drugmobile and the other half was still filing out.

"Don't know what you're talking about," I mumbled. Where was Mr. Burkett? What was taking him so long? Dewey wouldn't try anything with Mr. Burkett right there.

Right on cue the old reliable stomach started to knot up. I couldn't walk away because there was no place to walk to. Dewey would follow me, everyone would see me running from him, and they would hear whatever it was Dewey would yell after me.

"Everybody knows you like cocaine, Childish. Cocaine *Siegelman*."

Coco whirled around to face Dewey. He was roaring with laughter at his lousy joke. The other kids stopped milling around and got very quiet.

61

Where was Mr. Burkett? Most of the class was standing around waiting for him but he still hadn't come down the little steps. Were he and Detective Nark sharing a friendly joint in there, or what?

"Bet you'd like to sniff Cocaine Siegelman, wouldn't you, Childish? Huh, wouldn't you?" Dewey cracked himself up. There were a few nervous giggles from the audience.

Just a small hole in the ground, I prayed. Just big enough for me to fall into and disappear, right now.

"You stop calling me that!" Coco snapped. Her eyes were flashing. I'd never seen Coco's eyes flash before. She really *was* beautiful when she was angry.

Why am I thinking these things? Why *now?* How am I going to get out of this? *Where is Mr. Burkett?* He must be chatting with Detective Nark. Terrific. I hope they're having a nice chat; meanwhile, my life is about to go up in smoke, with the entire class here to laugh over my ashes.

Dewey bent down and stuck his nose next to Coco's cheek. "I don't mind sniffing Cocaine." He made loud sniffing noises.

What is he doing? How can I let him do that to Coco? Why am I just standing here? Now he was sniffing at her neck. He had one gorilla hand on her shoulder. Everyone was giggling and poking each other. *I have to do something.*

But what? He'll kill me if I try and stop him. He'll wipe me out in front of the whole class. Detective Nark might arrest him after he finished decorating the school yard with parts of my body, but I

62

wouldn't get too much satisfaction out of that after I was dismembered.

I cleared my throat. "Uh, stop it, will ya, Dewey."

It came out weak and skinny, just like me.

"Huh?" He started to turn around to see the chicken that made the squeaky little protest.

"He said cut it out, Dewey!" Coco cried. She reached up and clipped him on the nose. "Don't you come near me and don't you call me that again! It's not funny."

Dewey grabbed his nose. I swear, I think tears came to his eyes.

"Hey! That hurts! Hey, what'd you do that for?"

Just at that moment Mr. Burkett came out of the Drugmobile. The whole class was standing around laughing — at Dewey, for a change. Coco's eyes were still flashing, and she stood with her hands on her hips, as if she was daring Dewey to touch her again.

And he didn't. He just stood there, holding onto his nose.

Did anyone but me realize what just happened? They really did seem to be laughing at Dewey. But, didn't anyone notice that I had made one pitiful attempt to stop Dewey from bothering Coco, and that not only was I too scared of him to do anything but squeak out a few words, but that Coco obviously didn't need to be rescued at all? That she was tougher and braver than I was?

"She hit me!" Dewey yelled to Mr. Burkett. "She *hit* me!" His voice was outraged.

Mr. Burkett looked from Coco — who is shorter than I am, which is plenty short — to Dewey, who, even bent over holding his nose, is only a little smaller than King Kong.

"*She*," Mr. Burkett said, "hit *you?*"

"She *did*. Right in the nose."

"Is it bleeding?"

Dewey looked at his hand. "No."

Mr. Burkett looked at Coco. "Next time," he said sternly, "pick on someone your own size."

I don't know how I made it till three o'clock. I was so embarrassed I couldn't look at Coco all day.

Every time I heard a giggle or a titter, I was sure someone was talking about what Dewey said about me liking Coco, or about how I was so scared of him that even a frail little girl like Coco could deal with his bullying better than I could.

On the way down the hall to the lunchroom, Lana and Barbara and Shirley Matson bumped into me accidentally on purpose.

"Ooh, excuse me," said Lana. "I'll bet you wish Coco would bump into you. I'll bet you wish you could bump into Coco." She giggled wildly, and Barbara and Shirley nearly fell against the walls laughing. It wasn't even so much what she said as the *way* she said it that made it sound so bad. My face must have turned beet red again. I was just glad that Coco hadn't heard it.

At lunch, Dewey came over to my table. I was sitting with Ray and Danny, who were still laughing at what Mr. Burkett said to Coco. I was trying to laugh with them, which was not easy.

All of a sudden, there was Dewey, looming over me like the Empire State Building. "How come you need a girl to fight your battles for you, Childish? Huh?"

"What?" I suddenly realized that, after all, it wasn't my battle. He hadn't called *me* Cocaine. What was he talking about? I was trying to fight Coco's battle. He was mixing it all up. It wasn't any of my business in the first place. I should never have tried to get involved — not even the little bit I did try.

So he had said I liked Coco. So what was so terrible about that? Everybody likes Coco. What's not to like?

I was immediately ashamed of myself for thinking that way. Coward thinking; chicken thinking. That was my whole problem in the first place.

I pushed my lunch away. My stomach couldn't face food any more than I could face Dewey. I hated him — I hated myself. I hated the way I was thinking. I even began to hate Coco, for being named Coco and triggering this newest attack.

"You got some army, Childish," Dewey sneered. "That little runt, Bix, and a skinny girl. When are you gonna stand up and fight on your own?"

"Who wants to fight?" I didn't look at him.

"Not you, that's for sure."

"Fighting never proves anything."

"Oh, yeah? It proves you're not a chicken."

I didn't have an answer for that one. It was the only thing Dewey had ever said that made sense. And besides, I was so busy hating myself I couldn't think straight.

I guess Dewey got tired of trying to shoot down a flea with an elephant gun, because the next minute he just lumbered away and left me alone.

Except I wasn't alone.

Danny and Ray and the other kids at the table were staring at me.

"You gotta fight him, Childs," Ray said firmly. "You can't let him get away with this forever."

"Uh, well, the thing is, see —"

"Yeah, yeah, I know, so he'll pulverize you. But after that, he won't bother you anymore."

After I was pulverized *nothing* would bother me anymore.

"Dewey's the one who should pick on someone his own size," said Danny.

"There isn't anyone Dewey's size," said Ray.

"Well, Jeff shouldn't have to fight him."

Thanks, Danny.

"Jeff's so skinny, Dewey'll break every bone in his body."

Thanks, Danny.

"Well, that Coco can sure take care of herself. No wonder ya like her. I'd want her on my side in a fight, boy. Ha ha!"

Even you, Ray? The whole world is laughing at me now.

Ha ha.

I made it down the stairs and out of the school yard in record time. I didn't stop to wait for Bix. All I wanted to do was get out of there, go home, and disappear from the face of the earth before nine A.M. tomorrow.

I managed to avoid Dewey; I don't know why. Maybe he'd had enough for one day. Or maybe God had decided *I* had.

"Hey, Jeffrey, wait up! Jeff, *wait*, will ya?"

Bix came puffing up and fell into step behind me.

"So, how's the old hero today?"

"Hero?" I stopped in my tracks. "Who told you?" Was even Bix making fun of me now?

"Mrs. Winchell. Don't you remember?"

Oh, Fletcher. No, in fact I hadn't remembered. It seemed like a long time ago that I had let myself feel — even for a little while — like a hero.

"Do me a favor," I said. I started walking, fast. Bix shifted his feet so he was matching my strides. "Don't ever call me that again."

"Why not?"

"Just don't."

Six

"Jeffie! Come on, get up! You'll be late."

This was the third time she had called me. This was the third time I hadn't answered.

I was still in bed. Eventually she'd have to come in and see why I was still in bed, and then she'd have to let me stay home from school because I was too sick to get up.

Maybe I wasn't actually physically sick, like with the flu, but everyone knows there are ways of being sick that are not physical. I was sick in my heart, sick in my feelings, sick of my life. I was sick of school, sick of Dewey, and sick of being humiliated. Maybe I didn't have a fever, or a rash, or an earache, but my kind of sickness doesn't show on the outside.

"Jeffie, what's the matter with you?" My mother

charged into my room. "Don't you know what time it is?"

"I don't know, Ma," I said in a weak voice.

"Get up! I called you three times!"

"I don't feel so good."

"Oh, dear. What's wrong? What hurts?"

She came over to my bed and put her hand on my head.

"My — uh — stomach. And I feel kind of weak and achy." Well, I had to say something. I didn't know how my mother would take the "sick on the inside" explanation.

"You don't have a fever."

See, that's the thing with mothers. They like visible proof that you're sick. They want *symptoms*. Since I couldn't explain about Dewey, I couldn't tell her about how my feelings were sick. If she did believe me, she'd probably haul me off to a psychiatrist. I didn't need a psychiatrist. All I needed was to move to a new school, or enough money to hire a hit man to waste Dewey.

I groaned softly. "Boy, do I feel rotten."

"Like you're going to throw up?"

"It's a definite possibility." It was, too. If she made me go to school, my stomach wouldn't be worth a plugged nickel. Just thinking about facing Coco, Dewey, Lana, and the rest of the class was making it tighten up.

"Should I help you into the bathroom?"

"Oh, no, Ma, I don't want to move."

"It's probably just a virus," she said. She sounded

70

sympathetic. "I'd better stay home with you today."

Oh, no! She hadn't stayed home with me when I was sick for almost two years now. If she was home, I'd really have to stay in bed all day and keep up this act. And she'd come in every half hour with chicken soup and ginger ale and fuss over me. All I wanted, all I needed, was to be left alone. By *everyone*.

"That's all right, Ma. You don't have to. I can manage." I tried to sound sick but noble about it.

"But, honey, if you can hardly move —"

"Just put a pail by the bed in case I can't make it to the bathroom."

"I don't know . . ."

"I'll be okay. And it's the day before deadline and everything."

"Oh, I forgot. You're right. I just can't stay home today."

"I know, I know. Don't worry about me."

"I feel terrible about leaving you like this. Look, I'll make some Jell-O before I go. It'll be ready in a couple of hours. If you feel like eating —"

I groaned dramatically. "Please, don't talk about food."

"All right, honey. But if you feel better and get hungry —"

"I know what to eat. I just don't want to talk about it."

"Okay, okay. I'll leave a list of things you can eat on the kitchen table. I'll call you from the office later. No, wait, maybe I'd better not. I don't want you to have to get out of bed if you don't feel like it.

71

Look, why don't you call me? If you get up to go to the bathroom or something, give me a call and tell me how you're feeling."

"All right."

Finally she was gone. I heard the sound of the car pulling out of the driveway and breathed a sigh of relief. I didn't know how long I could go on being sick, but at least I had this one day of freedom. I didn't want to think any further than that.

THE REVENGE OF THE INCREDIBLE DR. RANCID AND HIS YOUTHFUL ASSISTANT, JEFFREY. *Continued.*

"He has been lucky, so far," said Dr. Rancid. "He has a certain sly cunning, but he is basically a stupid person and he cannot have good luck forever."

"Right," said Jeff. "Dumb luck is all. And it'll have to run out sometime."

"I think," Dr. Rancid said with a satisfied smile, "that time has come. I want to show you something."

Jeff followed Dr. Rancid to a wall safe which was hidden behind a movable bookcase. At a touch of a secret button, the bookcase swung out from the wall and exposed the safe. Only Jeff and Dr. Rancid knew the combination to the safe. It was in there that the brilliant doctor hid his most secret formulas, his most dangerous chemicals, his enormous pile of ready cash, etc.

Dr. Rancid twirled the combination lock and opened the safe. He took out a steel box, opened it, and showed Jeff what seemed to be a gun. But it

72

was a gun different from any Jeff had ever seen before, and Jeff was practically an expert on guns.

"What is that?" asked Jeff. "I've never seen anything like it."

"Of course you haven't. There's never been anything like it before. It will revolutionize modern warfare. And if it falls into the wrong hands it would mean disaster, destruction, and doom for the free world as we know it."

"It's much heavier than a regular gun," Jeff said, lifting it out of its box.

"That is because it is nothing like a regular gun," Dr. Rancid replied. "You will be careful with that?" he said nervously.

"I am always careful," Jeffrey said.

"Of course you are, my boy. That is one of your most valuable qualities. Any idiot can rush around waving his arms and yelling and threatening people; but to work for me you must be a cautious, patient planner capable of outwitting your enemy on a mental level."

"That shouldn't be too hard with Dewey," chuckled Jeff.

"Exactly. Now, I'll leave the planning part of it up to you. But when you do find him, this is the weapon of his destruction. It's a pulverizer gun and my latest invention."

"How does it work?"

"It's a variation on the disintegrator gun you see in science-fiction movies. I took off from that idea, but made certain refinements. You see, the pulverizer gun does not merely make people disintegrate, it actually pulverizes them."

"What's the difference?"

"Ahh. The difference is that a disintegrator gun would simply cause all the atoms of the body to separate and disappear. But my pulverizer gun first makes the body crumble, then mashes all the crumbled bits into a fine powder, thin as sand."

Dr. Rancid smiled, almost evilly.

"So the victim sort of gets mashed to death? Terrific." Jeff thought of Dewey. "That must hurt a lot."

"Yes. But only for the briefest instant."

"Too bad," said Jeff. "Maybe you can work on that."

"It's true. Dewey Belasco deserves more than an instant of pain. But there is no time, Jeffrey. While he is at large, we are not safe, and while we are not safe, the world is not safe. We must do our work without the constant threat of Dewey Belasco hanging over us."

"Yes, I know," said Jeff. "Oh, well, you can't have everything. You'd better show me how this works."

Dr. Rancid chuckled. "You mean, you've been holding it all this time and you haven't figured out how to use it yet? I'm surprised at you, Jeffrey."

Jeff smiled modestly. "Actually, I think I've got the principle of it, but we can't afford any mistakes. And none of us is perfect."

"You are right. We *cannot afford any mistakes*. Let me show you how to use the gun."

I was so relaxed not having to face school and working on "Dr. Rancid" that I actually felt pretty

74

hungry by eleven o'clock. I went into the kitchen and found my mother's list of things to eat. *Jell-O. Chicken broth — use the little packets. Toast and jelly. Ginger ale. Tea. Feel better. Love, Mom.*

I was in no mood for chicken broth and tea. I ate the entire bowl of Jell-O and was still hungry, so I made myself a bologna sandwich. Maybe my heart was sick, but my stomach hadn't felt this good in weeks.

Just before I went back to my desk, I remembered to call my mother. I told her I was okay and I hadn't thrown up. I didn't want her to do anything drastic, like call the doctor. I said I was still weak and achy and was getting right back into bed.

She sounded pretty concerned, which made me feel guilty for lying about this whole business; but the way I saw it, there was nothing else I could do. Short of telling her and my father the whole thing, which was out of the question. They'd both be a lot happier thinking I had a little stomach virus than knowing that their son was a sniveling coward.

At three-thirty the phone rang. I took my time answering it, thinking it might be my mother, who would expect me to crawl out of bed and limp to the phone.

"Hello?" I tried to sound pale.

"Jeffrey? Is that you?"

It was a girl.

"Yeah." My guard went up. "Who is this?"

"It's Coco Siegelman."

Coco? Why was Coco calling?

"Oh, hi, Coco."

"You weren't in school today."

"Yeah. Right."

"Are you sick?"

Suddenly it all came back to me with a whoosh. Coco's voice reminded me that the school was still there, the kids were still there, *Dewey* was still there. I could make them go away in my mind for a day, but tomorrow would come and nothing would have disappeared except today. My feeling of freedom, my unclenched stomach, my day of relaxation, all were snatched away.

"Are you sick, Jeffrey?"

"I have this, uh, stomach thing."

"Oh, that's too bad. Like a virus?"

"Right, right."

In fact, my stomach was feeling worse by the minute.

"Are you throwing up and everything?"

"No. It's not too bad." I tried my brave voice. But that was dumb. Coco, of all people, knew I was not brave. I dropped it and talked in my usual voice. "Just nauseous and I have these aches." I didn't tell her about feeling weak. What if she said, "So what else is new?" Of course, she wouldn't, not Coco; but she might *think* it and I couldn't stand knowing she was even thinking it.

"Do you think you'll be in school tomorrow?"

Not if I can help it. "I don't know. Have to play it by ear, I guess." I'd heard my father say that.

"Well. I — uh — hope you feel better. We have

some math homework. Do you want me to tell you what it is?"

"No, I don't have my book home. I'll make it up when I get back. Thanks anyway."

"If you want, I could — I mean, maybe — uh, well, maybe you better get back to bed."

What had she started to say? What was it she could do? And why had she changed her mind?

"I hope I'll see you tomorrow," Coco said.

Unless we both meet at the top of a Swiss Alp, I hope you don't.

I went back to my desk.

Why had she called? Just to hear my voice? What had she started to say? It must have had something to do with the math homework. I'd said I didn't have my book home, and she said, "If you want, I could —" Maybe she was going to offer to get my book for me. Or bring over her book?

No! Why would she do that? But what else could she have meant? I couldn't think of any other possibilities.

Could it be that she actually did like me? Could it be Coco who had written the only nice thing in the slam book about me? Or was it just that Coco was a basically nice person, and she felt sorry for me?

That must be it. And it would explain the slam book stuff too. It wasn't that she liked me, she just felt sorry for me. Like she'd feel sorry for a scrawny, stray dog who came to her door looking hungry.

The thought of Coco liking me — I mean, *really* liking me — was ridiculous. Absolutely insane. And besides, I didn't want to think about Coco now — or school. Or anything else that Coco reminded me of. All I wanted to think about was . . .

THE REVENGE OF THE INCREDIBLE DR. RANCID AND HIS YOUTHFUL ASSISTANT, JEFFREY. *Continued.*

"I've got you now, Dewey!" Jeffrey said. "You might as well give up."

"You'll never take me alive!" Dewey shouted.

"Who wants to take you alive?"

Dewey was on a ledge of the eighty-sixth floor of the Empire State Building. Jeffrey had followed him out onto the ledge. What Dewey didn't know was that Jeff was wearing Dr. Rancid's special boots, which were equipped with little suction cups all over the soles. The suction cups made it possible for Jeff to walk right up the side of the Empire State Building if he wanted to. With those special boots on, standing on a ledge without falling off was mere child's play.

"Before I destroy you, Dewey —"

"You? Destroy me? Ha! Hahahahaha!" Dewey laughed wildly, like some kind of crazed maniac. Jeff realized right away that Dewey was hysterical with fear.

"You have one chance to save yourself. If you tell me where your evil assistant, Lana McCabe is, I *might* go easy on you."

Dewey grabbed at the window behind his back. He teetered on the ledge, but caught hold of the window frame before he fell. Jeff breathed a sigh of

78

relief. Nothing must happen to Dewey before he found out where Lana was.

"I won't tell you nothin', you skinny little punk. You just come over here and try and make me. I'll pulverize ya."

Jeff smiled knowingly. "It's you who's going to be pulverized," he said, taking out Dr. Rancid's new weapon, "if you don't tell me where Lana McCabe is."

"You don't scare me." But his voice shook.

"Let me tell you about this gun, Dewey. This is a pulverizer gun. What it does is, first it takes your body apart, and then it mashes you to death. It's extremely painful."

"Oh, yeah? There's no such thing as a pulverizer gun."

Jeff began walking toward him slowly. Dewey cringed against the window.

"Wrong again, Dewey. There *wasn't* any such thing, until a few weeks ago, when Dr. Rancid invented it. I'd like to demonstrate it for you, but the only thing I could use for the demonstration are these pigeons and the Chrysler Building over there, and I don't think it would be right to kill an innocent pigeon just to prove that this gun works. Not to mention the Chrysler Building, which is a very famous piece of architecture."

Dewey threw himself backward through the open window and fell into an office. He slammed the window shut. Jeff smashed the glass of the window with one boot, balancing easily on the other as he did so. Dewey cowered behind a desk as Jeff jumped lightly into the room.

"It's all over, Dewey," Jeff said. "Your reign of terror and intimidation is through. Tell me where Lana McCabe is and make it easy on yourself."

"All right, all right!" screamed Dewey. "She's waiting for me at the Grand Canyon. I said I'd meet her there after I finished you off."

"She's going to be disappointed. Where, exactly, is she waiting? The Grand Canyon is a pretty big place."

"Kozy Kanyon Kabins," cried Dewey. "Kabin 13. It's a motel. You can't miss it."

"I won't. And now . . ." Jeffrey raised the pulverizer gun and clicked off the safety catch.

"You promised!" screamed Dewey. "You promised not to kill me if I told you where Lana was!"

"I lied," Jeff said calmly. "For the good of the entire free world," he added. Dewey was still pleading as he pulled the trigger.

"I hate cowards," said Jeff.

Dewey's body seemed to fly apart and then dissolve into a little pile of dust on the carpet. He didn't even have time to let out more than a short scream.

"Good-bye, Dewey Belasco," Jeff said. "The world is a better place now that you aren't in it anymore."

Jeff tucked the pulverizer gun back under his belt. The office door opened and a beautiful woman came in. She stared at Jeffrey and then looked down at the pile of dust on the rug that used to be Dewey.

"I'm sorry," said Jeff, "that I got your rug dirty."

Seven

"How do you feel this morning, Jeff?"

Actually, what I felt was starved. My dinner last night was toast, tea, and chicken broth, and I had to pick at that so my parents would see I was still sick.

"Uh, not so good, Dad."

"What's wrong?"

"My — um — stomach still —"

"I mean, besides your stomach." He came over and sat down on the edge of my bed. "Your mother says you had a bologna sandwich yesterday."

How did she know? Holy cow, she *does* count the cold cuts!

"But last night at dinner you made a big production out of hardly being able to choke down a little

81

soup. For some reason you just don't want to go to school."

The understatement of the year.

"What is it, Jeff? Are you having problems?"

This was my chance. I could tell him about Dewey, tell him that I couldn't take any more bullying and humiliation, tell him I couldn't face another day of being picked on and laughed at — the class joke, the school coward.

And then what? Would he let me stay in my room for the rest of the year? Would we move to a new town? Would he go see Mr. Burkett and say, "You tell that Dewey Belasco to stop picking on my son, the coward"?

Or would he give me a pep talk about facing up to your enemies, standing up to a bully, fighting like a man? And then bend his head in shame when he realized that the reason I had a problem in the first place was because I couldn't do any of those things, and if I could, the problem would have been solved already without his advice.

It was hopeless. There was no way he could help me if I told him; and if I told him, the only thing that would change would be the way he felt about me. I couldn't stand that. Maybe the whole class knew what I was really like, but as long as I could, I would keep my parents from finding out. That way, no matter what I went through in school, for a couple of hours a day there would be at least two people who thought I was pretty special.

"Why don't you tell me about it, Jeff?"

"There's nothing to tell. For a while yesterday I felt a little better, so I had a sandwich. But I was sorry afterward. It didn't sit too well." I didn't want to tell him I was faking, not even now, not even when he was sure I was. I couldn't admit that to him either.

My mother came into my room still wearing her bathrobe.

"Jeffrey, if you're still not feeling well I think we'd better call the doctor."

"Aw, no, Ma. It's just a stomach virus. I don't need a doctor."

"Then I think," she said firmly, "you'd better get out of bed and get ready for school."

"Liz, there must be a reason he —"

I gave up. I threw the covers off me and sighed. "There's no reason for anything," I said sourly. "I still feel tired and weak, that's all. But if you're going to make such a federal case out of it . . ."

I dressed as slowly as I could. I heard my mother and father in their room. It sounded like they were arguing, but I couldn't make out the words.

I dragged myself into the kitchen. I wasn't starving anymore. Far from it. The thought of going to school had wiped out any thoughts of food. Where my stomach had felt empty just half an hour before, now there was that cold, hard stone instead.

My mother was in the shower and my father tried to get me to eat. I picked at a bowl of cornflakes; and this time I wasn't making a big production out of it. No acting, no faking; just no eating.

"Would you like a ride to school?" my father asked.

"Aren't you going to be late?" I looked at the clock. He was usually gone by this time.

"I'm catching the eight-thirty-three today. I can drop you off on the way to the station."

"No thanks. That's a little early for me." Besides, what if Dewey was there when we drove up? What if he started in on me the moment I got out of the car? If I couldn't tell my father what was going on, I certainly couldn't take the chance that he'd see it with his own eyes.

My mother walked him to the door as he left. I heard them talking softly, then the front door slammed, and my mother came into the kitchen.

"Your father's worried about you, Jeffie," she said, pouring herself a cup of coffee.

"I'm glad *somebody* is," I grumbled. "You're *supposed* to be worried when your kid is sick."

"You think I don't worry about you?" She sat down across from me. "You're always complaining I worry too much."

"About the wrong things," I muttered. I shoved the cereal bowl away.

"Then tell me what the right things are," she said softly.

I jumped up, nearly knocking the chair over behind me.

"Nothing!" I yelled. "Nothing! There are no right things! Except when I'm sick, and then you don't care!"

84

I was so angry I almost forgot that I wasn't sick. After all, I said I was sick. What if I really was? She was sending me to school anyway, just as if she didn't care whether I had a relapse and got even sicker.

And once I started yelling, I couldn't stop. Anger seemed to grow in me till I felt like a volcano that's been quiet for years and then suddenly erupts, spilling hot lava over everything in its path.

"Even when I'm sick you don't stay home with me! Some stupid kid doing a pole vault is more important to you than me!"

Her face seemed to crumple. I backed away, shocked at what I had said. I hadn't meant to say it — I didn't even know I was *thinking* it till it came out of me, like the lava.

"But you never want me to stay home with you. You always tell me to go to work."

"Because I know you have to, and you want to." All the anger was gone now; I felt drained and exhausted and miserably sorry that I had said anything at all.

"I have stayed home with you sometimes," she said. "When you were really sick. And so has your father." Her voice was practically a whisper.

"I know, I know. I didn't mean it, Mom. I never meant to say it."

"You must have," she said, "or you wouldn't have said it. I can't believe that you don't know you're the most important thing in the world to me. I thought you understood."

"I do understand." I felt worse than I'd ever felt in my life. Worse even than the day before yesterday. I thought she was going to cry. I knew I would, in a minute.

I kept thinking that I never would have said those things to her, never would have felt those things, never *had* felt them before the trouble with Dewey started.

Before Dewey came into my class, it never bothered me that my mother was a sports editor. In fact, I thought it was kind of neat. Being the only woman sports editor in the county made her special; different from other mothers who were just teachers or social workers or lawyers.

It wasn't until Dewey started hounding me that I realized I was a weakling, and it wasn't until I realized that I was a weakling that I began to resent my mother's job. It's not that I minded her working. If she had been a teacher or a social worker or a lawyer, I bet I wouldn't have said any of those rotten things to her. But because I couldn't stand up to Dewey, her sports writing and her natural athletic ability made it seem like my mother was more *macho* than I would ever be.

Maybe I didn't have a stomach virus, but I had a virus. Dewey was the virus, I realized, and he was infecting every part of me, every corner of my world. Only this morning I'd thought I could keep Dewey out of my house. I thought I could almost live a double life, with one set of people not knowing what I was doing with the other set of people. I thought I could keep one side of my face turned toward my parents so they would never see the other cheek I kept turning every time Dewey conked me.

But it didn't work. It couldn't work anymore. By trying to keep them from finding out what I was really like, I'd hurt my mother a lot more than I would have if she'd known what was bothering me.

"I have to go to school, Ma. I'm going to be late. I really didn't mean it." I bent down and kissed her, something I haven't done voluntarily since I was nine.

"Talk to me, Jeffie. Whatever it is, please talk to me." She grabbed hold of my hand and held it tightly. I felt embarrassed and ashamed.

"I will, Ma," I mumbled. "Tonight. But I have to go now."

I left her sitting at the kitchen table, looking down into her coffee cup.

Bix was waiting outside the door.

"We're going to be late, Jeff. What took you so long? What was the matter with you yesterday? You should have called me. I could've looked it up in my first-aid cards."

"I had a stomach virus."

Bix was silent for a moment. "I don't think I have viruses in my first-aid cards. But I sent away for these medical cards. I bet they'd have stomach virus. They're really neat. They come in a black plastic simulated-leather file box shaped like a doctor's bag. I just sent for them though. I don't know when they'll come. But I can look up your stomach virus when I get them."

"Yeah, well, thanks, Bix, but I'm over the virus now."

I'm over one virus, I thought. The one I never really had. I don't know when I'll get over the other one.

I don't know what happened inside me as I walked to school. I know something happened, but I still don't know what it was.

I felt tired, I remember that. Tired of Dewey, tired of running, tired of feeling rotten about myself, tired of pretending in front of my parents. I also think I felt something like determination, like you're making a New Year's resolution that you really mean to keep. Thinking about it now, I remember that after I felt the tiredness, it almost seemed as if my back got straighter and my stomach got hard — not like there was that rock in it, though. This was a totally different feeling.

I walked into the classroom. Everyone else was already there. Mr. Burkett was writing something on the chalkboard.

"Feeling better, Jeff? Did you bring a note?"

"Yeah, I'm fine. I forgot the note. I'll bring it tomorrow."

He went back to the chalkboard.

Dewey stuck his foot out to trip me as I started up the aisle to my desk. I saw it just in time.

"What was the matter with you yesterday, Childish? Diaper rash?"

Lana and Barbara Boyle giggled like twin morons.

"I had a virus," I said pleasantly. "I got over it." I stepped across Dewey's foot. "But you'll never get over what you've got."

Dewey pulled his foot back under his desk. "Oh, yeah?" he said menacingly. He scowled at me. My stomach didn't clench, not one little bit. In fact, it felt fine. *I* felt fine. "Oh, yeah? What've I got?"

"Incurable stupidity." I flashed him a big grin and took my seat. I didn't really want to sit down; I suddenly had the most incredible feeling that if I tried to, right now, I could *fly*.

Ray guffawed loudly and slapped my back. Lana and Barbara turned around and stared at me. Danny was laughing so hard I thought he was going to bust. Mr. Burkett had his back to the class, but I swear his shoulders were shaking with laughter.

Dewey kept glaring at me. I ignored him.

I dropped my books on my desk. "Hi, Coco," I said cheerfully.

She looked nervous. "Oh, Jeff, he'll get you for that."

"I bet he will."

"You shouldn't have said that," she whispered. "He'll beat you up."

I nodded. "To a pulp, probably."

She shook her head. "It's not worth it."

"Oh, yes, it is, Coco." Maybe I couldn't stand up

89

and fly around the room, not with Mr. Burkett standing right up front, but *inside* I was soaring like an eagle. "It definitely *is* worth it."

For most of the morning I kept feeling I must be crazy. I was not *afraid.* I kept feeling not afraid, and knowing that I should be scared out of my pants at the prospect of Dewey beating me to a pulp at the first opportunity. Since I should be afraid and I'm not, that must mean I'm nuts.

I finally told myself that if I *was* nuts, I was also the happiest I'd been in months. It was almost as if I was looking forward to being beaten to a pulp. If that's not crazy, I don't know what is.

At one point I decided, okay, I'm crazy, and that's when I began to hum "Boom, boom, ain't it great to be crazy" under my breath. Coco was probably ready to call the men in the white coats when I started that. I hoped she wouldn't. I couldn't wait for lunchtime. That's when he'd get me. Or try to.

Fine. I was ready.

And no one was more surprised at that than me.

"I'm proud of ya, Childs," said Ray. He sounded almost fatherly.

I sat down next to him at the lunch table.

"Ya got a good one on him. 'Course, he'll smear ya all over the school yard for it."

"I guess so. Boy, am I hungry." I ripped the cellophane off my crackers so hard they crumbled in my hands. Then I dove into my clam chowder. I was *starved*.

I looked around between spoonfuls. Where was Dewey? I didn't see him anywhere. Maybe he was still on the lunch line. I wished he would hurry up and eat. I could hardly wait for the attack.

Boom, boom, ain't it great to be crazy . . .

"You better stay away from him," said Danny. "He's not used to people talking back to him."

"Then it's about time he got used to it." I wolfed down the grilled-cheese sandwich.

"Jeff, don't be stupid. Just avoid him for a few days and maybe he'll forget about it. You can't take him; you know it and I know it —"

"And he knows it," I finished. "Okay, so I can't take him. But I mean, I *really* can't take him anymore. I've had it, know what I mean? I've had it up to here with him."

"But he'll kill you!"

"If he kills me, my troubles will be over. If I kill him, my troubles will be over. Either way I win."

Danny looked at me gravely. "You know what? I think you're crazy, Jeff."

"I think you're right," I agreed.

After I finished eating I went out to the school yard with Ray and Danny. Still no sign of Dewey. Whatever it was that I'd felt walking to school, and calling Dewey stupid and waiting for him to come after me, was disappearing. Suddenly I was not feeling cheerful. Suddenly I was not feeling *not*

91

afraid. Suddenly I was not looking forward to being beaten to a pulp. Suddenly, my backbone, which had felt so stiff and straight on the way to school, had turned into a strand of limp spaghetti.

Well, I thought, at least I'm not crazy anymore.

On the other hand, crazy felt better.

"Here he comes," said Danny.

Just in time, too. In another minute I might have gone back to being completely sane, and run like hell.

Dewey came lumbering up to us. A respectful distance behind him were Lana McCabe, Barbara Boyle, Shirley Matson, and some of the other kids in the class.

"I been lookin' for you, Childish."

Just like a western movie. I nearly laughed. Except, it might have come out like a nervous giggle.

"You didn't look very hard," I said.

"You better," said Dewey threateningly, "take back what you said."

Take it back? What was going on here? Didn't he want to beat me to a pulp? If I said I was sorry, would that be the end of it?

Oh, sure. That might be the end of it for today. And he would have bullied me into humiliating myself in front of the whole class again.

Bix came puffing up to our friendly little group. "Hiya, Jeffie," he said, his eyes shining. "You gonna get him now?"

"Don't call me Jeffie," I said out of the corner of my mouth.

"Oh, boy!" Bix looked so excited I figured he must have his first-aid cards with him.

"Are you gonna take it back?" Dewey said.

"No. Why should I?" What was this? Some kind of kiddie game?

"I don't like to be called stupid."

"I don't like to be called Childish."

"Yeah, well, that's what you are."

I shrugged. "Okay. And stupid is what you are." We sounded like a couple of nursery school kids arguing in the sandbox. I couldn't believe this.

"If my name was Dewey Belasco," Bix piped up, "I wouldn't go around calling other people names."

"*Bix, shut up!*"

Dewey turned around slowly, his face darkening with anger.

"What did you say, shrimp?" He advanced on Bix, who didn't move from my side.

"I said, if my name was Dewey Belasco I wouldn't call other people names."

"Bix, will you *please* —"

"Why not?" Dewey demanded, his voice dangerously soft.

"Because they might start calling me a name. Like Doody Bigasso."

Everybody but Dewey and me laughed.

"Bix, are you *crazy* —"

"Doody Bigasso, Doody Bigasso!" sang Bix at the top of his lungs.

Dewey's eyes narrowed. He stuck out his ape arms and grabbed Bix by the shoulders. He shoved him up against the wall.

"Hey, leave him alone!" I yelled. "He's a little kid!"

"Yeah, leave him alone," said Ray. "You gonna let a little kid bother you?"

Coco, who had appeared from nowhere, started yelling too. "You big bully! You big bully!"

Bix didn't look one bit scared. He seemed to be enjoying the whole thing.

"Nobody calls me names," Dewey said.

"You can dish it out," said Bix, "but you sure can't take it."

Oh, brother.

Dewey's arm went back, almost in slow motion. Everyone started yelling at once. Before I knew what I was doing, before I had time to think, I flung myself onto Dewey's back with a "HII-YAH!" that must have sounded like Woody Allen trying to imitate Bruce Lee. All I knew was that Dewey was about to demolish a little kid, who happened to be the only kid in the world I could call a real friend.

I grabbed Dewey's arm. He tried to shake me off, but I held on like Scotch tape. He turned away from Bix, raised his other arm, and clipped me on the shoulder.

My knees buckled, but I didn't fall all the way down. I didn't think my shoulder was broken, but they could take X rays later. I wasn't sure I could move that arm, so as I staggered to my feet, I raised the other arm and punched Dewey in the stomach.

"Oof." He grabbed at his stomach and stepped back a little way. "You little creep!"

While he was still stepping back I pressed my advantage, and swung my fist in the general direction of his chin.

I didn't reach his chin, so my punch landed somewhere in his rib cage.

"Come on, Jeff! You got him going now!"

All around us kids were yelling, "Fight! Fight!" I was dimly aware of people running from all directions to see what was happening. Bix was shrieking at the top of his lungs, "Go, Jeffie! Go, Jeffie!" I wished briefly that he wouldn't call me Jeffie. Not at a time like this.

Dewey slammed me a good one in the chest that sent me reeling. I was not at all sure my collarbone wasn't broken, but they could X ray that later too. My shoulder and my chest were screaming in pain, and Dewey hadn't even gotten started yet.

He had to reach down in order to punch me in the face, which he was obviously eager to do. As he lowered his head, I socked him right in the mouth. It would have been a lot more satisfying if I hadn't bloodied my knuckles on his teeth.

He howled with rage, but I'm sure my hand hurt worse than his teeth. He didn't stop for any longer than it took him to howl, and the next thing I knew his fist connected with my nose and I was the one howling. My eyes filled with tears, and the pain was worse than anything I'd ever felt before.

I waved my arms around wildly, unable to see anything except tears and stars, and I felt another blow as Dewey bashed me right above the belt. I doubled over, clutching my stomach. This time, when my knees buckled, the rest of me followed.

"BREAK IT UP! BREAK IT UP!" My forehead was on the ground, my arms wrapped around my stomach. Something was gushing out of my nose. If I could see anything, I was sure I'd be looking into a pool of blood on the ground.

"You two come with me!" the voice said.

Coco and Ray and Danny knelt down next to me.

"Good going, Childs!" said Ray. He patted me on the shoulder.

"Not that shoulder, please," I groaned.

"Oh, Jeff, are you all right?" Coco's voice was shaky.

"No."

"You really gave it to him, Jeff!" Bix crowed.

"Is he bleeding?" I gasped.

"Not as much as you are." For some reason, Bix sounded proud of that.

"Lemme help you up, Jeff," said Danny. He and Ray each took one arm and hauled me to my feet. I groaned in pain. A teacher was standing next to Dewey, holding on to one of his arms.

"Both of you come with me!" she repeated.

"You got a stretcher?" I choked. My nose might be broken too. I wondered if you had to wear a cast on your nose when you broke it. I hoped not.

I was beginning to be able to see now.

"You saved my life, Jeff!" Bix yelled. "He saved my life," he told the teacher. "Doody was going to beat me up and Jeff stopped him."

"There will be no fighting on school grounds," the teacher said firmly. "I'm taking you two to see the principal."

"But he saved my life!" Bix insisted. "Look at how little I am! He would have killed me if Jeff hadn't saved my life."

Everybody started yelling at once, trying to tell the teacher that Bix was right, that Dewey was picking on a little kid and that that was the only reason I was fighting him. I just stood there, bleeding, throbbing, and listening to nearly a hundred kids being on *my side*. How, I wondered, could I feel so good when I felt so horrible?

We made it to the principal's office, but by the time we got there my handkerchief was filled with blood. Dewey was bleeding a little around the mouth, I was pleased to see, but other than that he looked ready to go another fourteen rounds.

My body, from my nose to my stomach, felt like one aching mass of broken bone. I was sure I needed a hospital more than I needed a lecture from the principal, but I guess that's not the way it works in our school.

The teacher who broke up the fight (and why couldn't she have come five minutes sooner?) ushered us into the principal's office.

"These two," she said in a tight, outraged voice, "were fighting in the school yard."

I took that as a compliment. Dewey was doing most of the fighting. What I was doing, mainly, was bleeding.

97

"You," Mr. Campbell said to me, "look like you ought to see the nurse."

At *least* a nurse, I thought. Until the ambulance comes, anyway.

"You know there's no fighting allowed on school grounds. Now, what was this all about?"

"He called me stupid," Dewey said sullenly. "Nobody calls me stupid and gets away with it."

"He was beating up on a third grader," I said. "If that isn't stupid, I don't know what is."

"See! He's doing it again!" Dewey cried.

"Now, boys," said Mr. Campbell, "sticks and stones may break my bones, but names —"

I don't believe this is happening. I am standing here, bleeding to death, with possibly a broken shoulder, a busted collarbone, and multiple internal injuries, and Mr. Campbell is giving us more sandbox wisdom.

"Name calling is silly and childish and you're both too old to get into fistfights over it. And you, Dewey —" obviously Dewey was an old acquaintance of the principal " — you ought to be ashamed of yourself, picking on a third grader. You've been in here enough times for fighting, but I'm really shocked that the strongest boy in the whole school would have to use his fists against a small child."

I think Dewey actually looked a little ashamed.

Mr. Campbell turned to me. "Where is the boy? Is he hurt?"

"No, he's fine." I cleared my throat. "I stopped it in time."

"Well, that's all right, then."

What's all right? Not me. I'm going to keel over in about a minute.

"You'd better see the nurse," Mr. Campbell said. "And you," he said grimly to Dewey, "had better stay here and have a little talk with me. But first, I want you two to shake hands and agree not to fight anymore."

You've got to be kidding. Dewey and I just stood there. His arms dangled at his sides in their usual gorilla fashion. Mine didn't move because I wasn't sure I could move them.

"Come on, now. Shake hands and apologize to each other."

This was unbelievable. Dewey stuck out his hand and grabbed mine. He didn't look at me. I suppressed the urge to scream "OUCH!" as my shoulder throbbed with pain.

"'M sorry, toadface," he mumbled.

"I'm sorry I didn't knock your teeth out, pigeon-brain," I replied under my breath.

"There, that's better." Mr. Campbell beamed with satisfaction. He was either deaf, crazy, or just extremely anxious to have this truce settled before I bled all over his desk.

"Now you two can be friends."

Oh, yeah. Bosom buddies.

"You'd better get down to the nurse's office; see if she can get that bleeding stopped."

I think it was beginning to stop on its own by now, but I was glad to get out of there and get some medical attention. Danny and Ray were waiting on a bench outside the office.

"We'll take you down to the nurse," said Danny. "You look rotten."

"I feel worse than I look."

"But you did it," said Ray. "You finally did it. I'll bet he won't want to fight you again."

"God, I hope not."

The nurse said my nose wasn't bleeding anymore and she cleaned me up some. She felt my shoulder and my chest and said she didn't think anything was broken.

I didn't know how she could tell without X rays, but the truth was that they were beginning to hurt a little less and I could move my arm all the way around now, and my neck and head too. I wasn't sure about my nose, but even that was only sore now, and not screaming with pain.

"Why don't you stay here and just rest awhile," she said. "If you don't feel better in half an hour or so, we'll call your mother to come and get you."

I didn't even stay half an hour. As the various parts of my body gradually began to feel merely semi-terrible instead of agonizing, I got more and more eager to return to class. Finally I told the nurse I was feeling okay and she gave me a pass and sent me on my way.

I don't know if I'll ever again feel as terrific as I felt when I walked into that classroom. As I opened the door and came in, Mr. Burkett stopped explain-

100

ing fractions and turned to see who it was. As he did, Danny, Ray, and practically the whole class started clapping and cheering and yelling, "Yeah, Jeff!" It was incredible. When was the last time you saw the loser of a fight get a standing ovation?

I just stood there, not believing my ears, not believing my eyes, just feeling like all my aches and pains were being washed away by this ocean of friendly cheers. If I smiled any wider or any longer, my mouth would have started aching along with the rest of me.

I took a deep breath — or tried to. It hurt to breathe in. I nodded modestly.

"Okay, okay, that's enough," said Mr. Burkett finally. "Sit down, Jeff."

I slid into my seat next to Coco. Ray reached over, his arm raised. I turned around as fast as I could. "Hey, not on the shoulder, okay, Ray?"

"Got ya, killer."

Coco looked at my face. For an awful moment I thought she was going to cry.

"Oh, Jeff, you look terrible! I thought you were going to bleed to death."

"So did I," I said lightly. I bent down to reach into my desk for my math book and caught Lana McCabe staring at me. She looked away quickly, the minute she noticed I'd caught her looking. She probably couldn't believe I could still walk, let alone make it back for the rest of school.

Dewey slouched in a few minutes later. He handed a pass to Mr. Burkett and took his seat. No one snickered, no one said a word. They glanced at him for a second or two, then looked back to Mr. Burkett, as if they'd lost interest in Dewey's activities.

No standing O for the winner. It was hard to believe, but this crowd was on *my* side now.

I sat back in my chair and sighed. I didn't know what would happen tomorrow. I didn't even know what would happen after school today. But I had *this*. I'd stood up to the guy who'd been terrorizing me for months, and I'd lived to tell the tale.

Whatever happened next, I was no longer Childish the Chicken.

Eight

Nothing happened next.

I walked out of school with my head high, even walked slowly, in case Dewey was looking for me. But he wasn't. He was nowhere in sight. (I was also walking slowly because I still couldn't take very deep breaths. Dewey must have gotten me right in the solar plexus.)

Lana, Barbara, and Shirley walked past me out of the school yard, and Lana and Shirley sort of nodded good-bye to me. *Didn't say a word*. Barbara smiled and waved cheerily. "See you Monday, Jeffie."

It was wild. Was it really going to be like in the movies? Was I really free, now that I had stood up to The Bully? Well, maybe I wasn't going to be free from Dewey, but at least I was going to be free *inside*, knowing that I could no longer call myself a coward, and neither could anyone else. I sincerely hoped — *prayed* — that I would never have to fight Dewey again, but I was convinced that I would do it if I had to. And maybe, now that Dewey was convinced of that, he wouldn't be so eager to get me to fight him. Not that he was afraid of me. I didn't believe that for a minute. After all, I was the one who lost all the blood, as well as the fight. But maybe he'd be bored with me now that he didn't think I was afraid of him anymore. After all, there's no point in trying to terrify someone you know isn't going to be terrified.

I whistled as I walked along.

"Hey, Jeffie, you're a hero again!" Bix yelled. He ran up to me. "First you saved Fletcher's life, now you saved mine! You're a *double* hero! Thanks a lot, Jeff."

"Listen, Bix, you stay away from him," I warned. "He might still have it in for you."

"Ah, I'm not afraid of him. Not as long as you're around."

"Uh, do me a favor, Bix. Don't count on me to save you again. I don't know if my body can take it. Anyway, you should have stayed out of it. It was my fight, not yours."

"But what are friends for?" asked Bix. "I stand up for you, you stand up for me."

Terrific. If he stood up for me any more, I might get killed.

"Come on over my house," Bix said. "I'll look up all your injuries in my first-aid cards."

See, I knew it!

"Okay, okay. But you better not try and put my nose in a sling."

My parents were both home by the time I got in from Bix's. I still looked pretty terrible, as Bix's mother had told me, although I was feeling a lot better. My nose was swollen, my pants were ripped at one knee, and my left arm was hanging kind of funny. A lot better? I was feeling terrific.

They went into instant frenzy. They were all over me, and before I could say a word, my mother was yelling into the phone at the doctor, making him promise to wait in his office until we got there.

"*What happened to you?*" my father demanded, as my mother screamed at the doctor.

"I was in a fight. You should have seen the other guy."

"Worse than you?" my father asked incredulously.

"Not a mark on him." I looked at my bruised knuckles. "I did get him in the mouth, though. I might need a rabies shot."

"Is that why you didn't want to go to school today?"

"Actually, Dad, it's sort of a long story." Which, at last, I felt I could tell them. After all, the story had a happy ending. I didn't have to worry about their being ashamed of me anymore.

"And I promised to tell Mom all about it tonight anyhow."

"You can tell me about it," my mother said, "when we get back from the doctor. Now, where does it hurt?"

"Are you kidding? Where *doesn't* it hurt?"

Dr. Wicke said my nose was not broken and that I was very lucky it wasn't. He sent us down the hall to get some X rays taken, but he was pretty sure there wasn't anything else broken either. He said I'd probably hurt when I inhaled for a day or so, as that's what happens when you get hit in the solar plexus. He told my parents a few gruesome things to watch out for in the next couple of days; I think to make sure there weren't any major internal injuries.

We got back into the car and my mother turned around in the seat to look at me.

"Now," she said, as my father turned the key, "what in the world is this all about?"

"Like I said, it's a long story." I took as deep a breath as I could, sat back in the seat, and began to tell them about the last few months of my life.

I was still talking when we got home.

I was still talking while my father ran me a hot bath and my mother dished out some casserole she'd forgotten to take out of the oven in the general rush to the doctor's.

"So I really didn't mean what I said this morning. It sounds dumb, I guess, to pick on your job because someone's picking on me."

She looked almost sad. "People a lot older than you do the same thing. You can't help what you feel. I just wish you'd told us before. I hate to think all the time you were suffering without having anyone to talk to. You could have talked to us, Jeffie."

"But you couldn't have helped me," I said. "It was my own problem."

"Maybe we couldn't have helped you; we'll never know, one way or the other. But we would have *listened*. We would have understood what was making you unhappy. And we never would have thought you were a coward."

My father came in from the bathroom.

"There's a nice, hot bath waiting for you," he said, "which is exactly what my father prepared for me after I got beaten to a pulp."

"You got beaten to a pulp? When?"

"When I was twelve."

"What happened?"

He started slowly, as if he didn't want to tell me this at all. "There was this kid. He used to come up to me every day after school and say, 'Give me a quarter or I'll beat you up.' I kept giving him a quarter, when I had one. Sometimes I ended up going without lunch so I'd have a quarter to give him. To me, this kid looked like Goliath. And every time I gave him a quarter, he'd do something like rip my shirt, or grab my books and run, or try and pull my pants down. But he never beat me up, you understand."

My father's voice got lower as he talked. He had this faraway look in his eyes, almost like he was traveling back in time and living the whole thing over again.

107

"And when I told my father about how my clothes kept getting torn, and why I needed extra money all the time, and why I had to keep paying for the books Goliath took from me, he said he'd teach me to box so I could defend myself."

"That's what I thought you'd do with me," I said.

"Well, your mother might be a better teacher than I would."

I knew it, I knew it! Yet, how could anyone beat up my father? I couldn't imagine my father not being able to stand up for himself. Like I said, this was a guy who could handle *anything*.

"So my father tried to teach me to fight. Except, every time we had a lesson I ended up running to my mother, crying, because my father never could teach me to defend myself well enough to duck when he punched me in the nose."

"Your father punched you in the nose?"

"And the stomach. I don't think he really meant to, though. I just didn't know how to dodge the punches."

"That's terrible! And Grandma let him?"

My father shrugged. "She thought he was right. He kept telling me, 'A coward dies a thousand deaths, a brave man only one.' I kept telling him I'd rather be a live coward than a dead brave man. And he kept being ashamed of me and telling me I'd never be a man at all if I didn't learn to face up to a fight."

It sounded so awful when he was saying it that I began to wonder how I could have thought my father would say things like that to me.

108

"So I never would have called you a coward," my father said, as if he was reading my mind. "I really *would* have understood."

"But what happened? Did you —"

My father's voice got louder and firmer, like he was shaking off the bad memories and coming back in time to Now. "Everybody's a coward about something," he said. "Remember that. It's not cowardly to be afraid to fight somebody twice your size. It's normal. It's healthy. That fear is there for a good reason — to help keep you alive. It's nature's way of warning you about danger."

"But what happened with Goliath?"

"He beat me senseless," my father said briefly. "I didn't land one punch."

I didn't think he wanted to talk about it anymore. My mother patted him on the shoulder, almost like she was comforting him. It was hard to believe that after all these years, something that had happened to him as a kid still hurt so much. But I really thought it did.

"So you're saying I shouldn't have fought Dewey?" I was a little confused at this point.

"No. I'm just saying I know how you feel and I would have been the last person in the world to think you were a coward."

"But is it better to be a live coward than a dead brave man?" I asked.

"I don't know." My father shook his head. "I guess that's something you have to decide for yourself. Your bath is probably ice water by now," he added.

"Did he ever bother you again? After he beat you up?"

"No. He lost interest in beating up smaller kids when he took to stealing cars."

"You'd better get into that bath now, Jeff," my mother said. "And next time — whatever it is — please tell us about it. That's what we're here for."

She came around to the back of my chair and hugged me.

"Careful of my shoulder!"

Nine

Saturday afternoon, Matthew, Mark, Fletcher, and Bix came to shoot baskets. My shoulder was still bruised, so I was a little off, but I was doing okay. Fletcher is too little to shoot baskets, so I managed to lift him up a couple of times and let him try to make a shot that way.

In the middle of a two-on-two game — Fletcher was supposed to be keeping score — Danny and Ray came pedaling up on their bikes.

"Hey, Childs, how ya doing?" Ray yelled.

"Hey, Ray."

They dropped their bikes on the sidewalk and jogged up the driveway.

"We just came to see how you felt," Danny explained. "Anything broken or anything?"

"Nah, I'm fine." I tossed up the ball, just to show

them how fine I was. It hit the backboard and bounced off the rim. Fletcher caught it as it came down.

"You missed!" he shrieked. "You missed, Jeffie."

"I know, I know," I muttered.

"How about a little game?" Ray made dribbling motions with his hands.

"Sure. We can have three on three."

"You mean, with them?" Ray said. "Aw, come on, they're little."

"Yeah, but they're okay," I said. "And besides, they were here already. I promised to play with them." What I didn't say was that they were here all along, when no one else was. When I thought I hadn't a friend in the world my own age, when I was sure my whole school either made fun of me or ignored me, Matthew, Mark, and Bix were always there, looking up to me as the "big kid."

"We're not little," Mark said. "We're just short for our age."

"Okay, okay," said Ray. "But not that one!" He pointed at Fletcher.

"He's the scorekeeper," said Bix. "He doesn't play."

"Can he keep score?" Danny asked doubtfully.

"Are you kidding?" snorted Matthew. "He can't even add."

"Oh, brother," Ray groaned. "This is gonna be some game."

That was putting it mildly.

Matthew yelled "FOUL!" every time Ray got near

112

him, and after yelling "FOUL!" six times, he insisted that Ray had fouled out of the game.

"No foul-outs," I told him. "This isn't the NBA, you know."

"But it's the rules," Matthew said. "If you don't stick to the rules I'm not going to play."

He stalked off down the block, leaving us with three against two. So Danny and Ray played against me, Bix, and Mark. Every time someone made a basket, Fletcher yelled out any number that came into his head.

"Three!"

"A basket is two points!" yelled Ray.

"Thirty-nine!" cried Fletcher, as Bix hit one.

"It's six to four!" Ray howled.

"Sixty-four!" Fletcher announced.

Within minutes after Matthew left, Danny and Ray were laughing so hard at Fletcher that they couldn't play.

"Game called on account of hysterics!" yelled Bix. He tossed the ball to Fletcher.

"Yay!" screamed Fletcher. "I win." He grabbed the ball in both arms and ran toward his house.

"Hey, that's my ball!" But I was laughing too hard to chase him.

Danny dropped to the grass, clutching at his sides. "This is the craziest game I ever played," he gasped.

Fletcher had already disappeared into his house.

"Come on," Bix said to Mark, "we'll get the ball back." They trotted off to the Winchells'.

113

"Hey, Jeff, look who's coming," Ray said. He plopped down on the lawn next to Danny. "Your girl friend."

I looked up. Coco was pedaling her bike slowly down the street, holding on to the handlebars with one hand and her black flute case with the other.

"She's not my girl friend," I muttered. "She's just a friend who happens to be a girl."

And what was she doing here *now?*

She stopped the bike next to our driveway.

"Hi, Jeff."

"Hi."

"Hi, Danny. Hi, Ray."

"Hi, Coco. Going for your flute lesson?"

"Yeah. I just stopped by to find out how you were feeling, Jeff. You looked so awful yesterday, all covered with blood and everything."

"Aw, he wasn't all covered with blood," Ray said. "Just his nose."

"Well, *I* thought he looked awful," Coco said. "I was worried about him."

I gulped. She'd been worried about me the day I stayed home from school with my fake stomach virus too.

"I'm — uh — fine."

Ray snickered. Danny jabbed him with an elbow.

"Oh, that's good." She came over and sat down next to me. Her hair was all shiny and she smelled like a flower. She was wearing jeans and a yellow T-shirt with "Coco" embroidered over her heart. I gulped again. I must have looked like a goldfish. For a moment, anyway, I thought I might not be getting enough air.

"And I wanted to show you something." She reached into her jeans pocket and pulled out an envelope. "Look at this."

Ray and Danny leaned over as I opened the envelope. It was an invitation to a party at Lana McCabe's house.

"You're going to be invited too," she said. "And you and you," she added to Ray and Danny.

"How do you know?" I asked.

"Lana told me. She's taking the invitations around herself. She'll probably be over later."

I looked at the envelope. "Siegelman" had a little circle dotting the *i*.

So it was Lana who had written those nasty things about me in the slam book — or some of them, anyway. I'd recognize those *i*'s anyplace. Why should she invite me to her party? Just because I finally tried to fight Dewey?

"It's probably a joke," I said. "About inviting me."

"It's no joke," said Coco. "She really is inviting you."

"I don't want to go to any party *she* gives," said Ray.

Coco turned to me. "You'll go, won't you, Jeff?"

Ray and Danny grinned at each other. They didn't say anything, but they leaned forward as if they couldn't wait to hear my answer. I began to feel really embarrassed.

"I still don't believe she's really going to invite me," I mumbled. "Why should she? She hates me."

"Oh, she doesn't hate you," said Coco.

I wondered if Coco had been sleepwalking all these months while Lana and Barbara and Shirley were sneering at me.

"She puts on a great act, then," I said.

Coco stood up. "Well, I have to go or I'll be late for my lesson. I hope you come to the party, Jeff. And you too," she added quickly, nodding toward Danny and Ray.

She rode off on her bike. Danny punched me in one arm, Ray in the other.

"ow!"

"I hope you come to the party, Jeffie," Ray said, in a high-pitched giggle. "Ooh, Jeffie, you *have* to come to the party."

"Cut it out," I said. My face was getting hot. I poked Ray in the ribs.

"Ah, leave him alone," Danny said. "You just wish she liked you instead of him."

"WHAAT?" yelled Ray. "Are you nuts? That's some joke! Ha ha!" He laughed loudly. For some reason it sounded like he almost had to force himself to laugh.

Coco was right. An hour later, after Danny and Ray had gone home for lunch, Lana came by.

"Oh, thanks," I said, sticking the invitation in my pocket.

"Will you come?" she asked.

116

"Well, I don't know."

"You better," she said. "Coco won't come if you don't, and Laurie won't come if Coco doesn't—"

So that's why she invited me! Coco made her! Maybe I should have felt insulted, but I didn't. I felt great. I felt so great my face began to get hot again, and I was afraid I was blushing. Coco did like me! I wasn't just imagining it. She *must* like me. But that was no reason to keep turning red all the time. How was I going to sit next to her in school every day if I kept blushing every time I looked at her or thought about her?

"But I might have invited you anyway," added Lana.

"Oh, sure. Thanks a lot."

"So will you come?"

"I'll see," I said carelessly. The picture of my fist connecting with Dewey's mouth, and his howl of pain, flashed through my mind, and I suddenly got this incredible feeling of power over her.

"I'll let you know."

"When?"

I smiled. *When I get good and ready*, I thought to myself.

THE REVENGE OF THE INCREDIBLE DR. RANCID AND HIS YOUTHFUL ASSISTANT, JEFFREY. *Continued.*

"Come on out, Lana!" Jeffrey called. "I know you're in there."

He pounded on the door of Kabin 13 at the Kozy Kanyon Kabins motel.

117

"It's all over, Lana. Give yourself up."

"You'll never take me alive!" Lana screamed from inside.

"That's what your friend Dewey said," Jeff answered. "And he was right. I didn't. He's dead, Lana. All that's left of him is a bunch of dust lying on a rug in the Empire State Building."

The door of the Kabin flew open and Lana stood there with a look of shock and horror on her face.

"Dead? He's dead? Oh, oh, then this really is the end of everything!"

She ran past Jeffrey, shrieking and screaming, and headed straight for the edge of the Grand Canyon.

But Jeffrey had been prepared for this. Coco was stationed at the edge of the canyon, armed with Dr. Rancid's tranquilizer gun. As Lana ran toward the edge, meaning to leap into the Grand Canyon and kill herself, Coco zapped her with the tranquilizer gun. Lana fell to the ground and just lay there.

Jeffrey ran over to Coco, who was leaning over Lana's limp body.

"Good work, Coco! Killing herself would have been too easy. She has to pay for her years of crime."

Coco and Jeffrey bent down to pick up Lana. Lana's eyes were open. She could hear everything, but she just couldn't move because of the tranquilizers shot into her.

"I never should have gotten involved with Dewey," Lana said tearfully. "I'm sorry for all the bad things I did. He made me do them. It was his evil influence. He kept telling me you were our enemy and you were too dangerous and powerful and had to be eliminated. I never had anything against you personally, Jeffrey. In fact, I always admired you."

"Well, you'll have plenty of time to think about that in jail," Jeff said. "We better get her to the plane and bring her in, Coco."

"Oh, Jeff," said Coco, "the whole world will be grateful to you for what you've done. You are the bravest person I ever saw."

"I just try to do my job, Coco," he said modestly.

"Oh, Jeffie," she sighed. She threw her arms around him and kissed him.

"Now, now, Coco, there's no time for that," he said firmly.

Coco blushed embarrassedly. "I'm sorry," she said. "I couldn't help it."

"I understand," said Jeff. "But business before pleasure, you know. Now, let's get this show on the road.

"We're moving out."

"THE END"

About the Author

Ellen Conford was born in New York City and now
lives in Massapequa, Long Island, New York with
one sheepdog, two cats, one son who is in college and
one husband who is a professor of English. She
started writing when she was in the third grade but
her first book wasn't published until after she was
grown up. She has published fifteen books for children
of all ages. She is the 1981 champion of Scrabble
Club #32, Massapequa, New York.

She is also the author of *Dreams of Victory*, available
in an Apple Paperback edition.